Surviving Gretchen
The Storms of Friendship (Book 1)

Bonnie Daly

Lune Spark Books, Morrisville, NC

Publisher: Lune Spark L.L.C.

PO Box 1443, Morrisville, NC, 27560, US

www.lunespark.com

Email: books@lunespark.com

Phone: +1 (919) 809-4235

Ordering Information: Quantity sales. Special discounts are available on quantity purchases by corporations, associations, and others. For details, contact the publisher at the address above.

Or visit www.lunespark.com

ISBN 13: 978-0-9974771-2-2

ISBN 10: 0-9974771-2-1

1. Middle Grade 2. Children 3. Relationships 4. Family

First edition (Update on Oct 21, 2017)

For Cameron

Surviving Gretchen

The Storms of Friendship (Book 1)

Prologue

The emergency room doors of Lakewood Hospital flew open while a team of medics rushed Emma in through a seemingly endless expanse of hallway. Her brother Keith and their dad hurried alongside them. Scared didn't even begin to describe the way Keith felt as his little sister laid so still on the stretcher. Emma was never still—not ever, he thought, staring down into her pale, lifeless face.

"We need a doctor here, stat! She's not responding!" one of the medics called out.

She's not responding played over and over again in his mind. He tried to shake it off, but the words haunted him. Quickly, Keith reached out to squeeze her hand, hoping beyond all hope she'd squeeze back. He found her hand limp and cold as ice, sending an involuntary shiver of fear down his spine. He needed her to wake up. Keith loved Emma more than he could say. The problem was, he never said it. All the teasing and tormenting he'd always put her through was his way of showing affection. He needed to tell her that but was afraid he might now never get the chance.

"Get her into room 2, NOW!" someone ordered.

As the medics turned the corner to wheel Emma into the room, a nurse suddenly appeared and halted Keith and his dad from going any farther. "I'm sorry, but you'll both have to wait out here," she said in a clinically cold yet sympathetic tone.

Keith was overtaken by intense emotions, while he and his dad stood outside the room watching the medical team working on his sister through the window. Dear God, please let her be okay—she's got to be okay, he silently pleaded. He may have been a spirited, confident sixteen-year-old, but at that moment he'd been reduced to a scared stiff, frightened little boy.

Their next door neighbor, Dr. O'Donnell—who was like a second father to Keith and Emma—was the doctor in charge. His daughter Abby, who'd been Emma's lifelong best friend these past fourteen years, had just showed up with her uncle. They'd both been there when it happened. Keith saw the depths of unfathomable sorrow on Abby's face and wished he could convince her it was all going to be okay. Yet, how could he convince her of that when he couldn't even convince himself?

Moments later, his mom showed up and Keith knew he needed to be strong for her. It ripped his heart out to see her hurting so. He was also aware of how hard his dad was trying to keep it together for their sake. The three of them huddled close, transfixed on the person they loved more than life itself, who was on the verge of losing her own life.

An eternity passed as they watched and waited. Suddenly, there was a surge of activity around Emma. "Dad, what's wrong—what's happening?" Keith asked, his voice sounding nothing like his own.

Just then a nurse flung open the door to ER room 2 and yelled out, "CODE BLUE! CODE BLUE! PATIENT'S GONE INTO CARDIAC ARREST!"

Chapter 1

The massive double doors of Lakewood Junior High School burst open with all the intensity of an explosion as the stampede of eager, screaming escapees shot forth from the scene of their academic confines. Summer was here, and the moment was charged with carefree contemplations, devious deliberations and mischievous mindsets.

"Hey, Abby! Over here!" Emma shouted, jumping up and down as she gesticulated wildly to capture her best friend's attention.

Abby eyed her across the pandemonium unfolding on the plush green grass of the school lawn and had to laugh; Emma's enthusiasm was not only contagious but at this moment made her look very much like an over-caffeinated capuchin monkey on a pogo stick. She waved back, then made her way through the tightly-woven group of students—who were quickly becoming unraveled in their newfound freedom—to where Emma awaited her under the canopy of a giant maple tree.

"Wow, you think you could at least *try* to act happy?" Abby teased.

Emma's big brown eyes blazed with excitement. Abby flung her backpack down on the ground next to Emma's. Overcome with glee, Emma squealed embarrassingly then tried the best she could to compose herself.

"We're gonna have the best summer ever!" Emma said, still trying hard to contain herself but not really succeeding as she was now jumping up and down again, her long brown hair flapping all around her. A few kids stifled laughter as they walked by, but Emma was oblivious.

"Indeed we will," Abby said, amused by her friend's antics.

Emma Rhodes and Abby O'Donnell had been inseparable best friends as well as next-door neighbors since the beginning of time—or at least time as they knew it over the past fourteen years. Emma was an impulsive ball of endearing energy one minute, then a shy, sensitive, sweet girl the next; whereas Abby was consistently outgoing with a slightly more mature, sensible demeanor than her overly-excitable, spontaneous counterpart.

Emma, attempting a serious stance, suddenly faked a British accent and said, "My dearest Abigail, it is of the utmost importance that we make a pact."

"Okay...about what?" Abby laughed at Emma's ridiculous accent, "must be quite serious for you to call me Abigail."

"It is completely serious, my dear girl," Emma said. "You and I must make an official proclamation which states we'll be inseparable for the entire summer."

Infected with Emma's fake accent germs, Abby replied, "A most excellent idea...however, we shall need to put it in writing."

"Why, of course. I'll write up a legally binding document for us this evening...I'll just have to make sure we both get a chance to sign it before my brother's goat eats it." They broke into giggles but continued on with their farce.

"Hmmmm...perhaps we'd better just shake on it, then," Abby said. They performed a business-like handshake, fell into a fit of laughter, then plunked themselves down in the grass.

"Emma, I am seriously psyched for tonight," Abby said, her big baby blues twinkling with excitement. "Dad says he and Uncle Clegg have everything all set up for the Rock the

Dock fundraiser—even the bonfire pit and the stage for your brother's band are ready for action." Abby pulled the elastic band out of her long, wavy strawberry blonde hair, allowing it to break free from its ponytail status.

"That's so cool!"

"I know, right? We're gonna have a blast! But, of course, we *will* have to endure Keith's band…" Abby said, making a face which quickly turned into a grin. "They really are quite good, just don't ever tell him I said that."

"Oh, believe me, I wouldn't dream of it. He's full enough of himself as it is."

That's certainly true," added Abby. They both smirked.

"It'll be so awesome to finally swim in that lake…I cannot stand the excitement!" said Emma, unexpectedly springing up like an unrestrained jack-in-the-box.

"Hold your excitement," Abby said, rising to her feet. "Dad says it's been forty years since anyone's used the beach, so it's pretty much trashed. But after tonight's fundraiser, along with all the help from the volunteers over the next few weeks, it should be in perfect shape for having a massive celebration on the Fourth of July."

"Our swim team's gonna love it!"

A pretentious prima-donna of a girl named Gretchen barged abruptly in between them. Her brightly-bleached, overdone hair was only upstaged by her severely out of place hot pink designer sundress. The smug look—permanently plastered on her face—clearly revealed everything else anyone would ever need to know about her.

With her back pointedly toward Emma, Gretchen addressed Abby.

"Speaking of the team, I am over the moon at being selected for your uncle's elite, exclusive swim team this summer! Mummy *assures* me that only the best of the best were chosen." She smiled winningly—overcome by her own snootiness—her nose so high in the air it was a wonder it wasn't capped in snow.

Emma leaned out past Gretchen into Abby's view and sneered while Abby did her best to keep a straight face.

"Ummmm…hey, Gretchen," Abby began, searching for the politest possible way to bring Gretchen back down to earth. "I'm happy you joined up as well. But it certainly isn't elite or exclusive, and no one gets selected for it, you just sign up. It's basically just a lot of fun for all us girls who love swimming."

Emma tried unsuccessfully to stifle a laugh. An indignant grimace scrawled its way across Gretchen's face as she whipped her head around to glare at Emma with her beady little green eyes. Emma provided her with mock innocence in return. Gretchen turned back to readdress Abby, her expression changing from condescending to congenial in less than a heartbeat.

"Oh nonsense! Anyway, Abby, I've been looking for you everywhere." Out of the corner of her eye, Gretchen noticed Emma moving over toward Abby and again purposefully placed herself in front of Emma.

Emma made an exaggerated eye roll, which wasn't lost on Abby who tried again not to smirk.

"Mummy insists that after the thing at the beach tonight you simply must come do a sleepover. You and I are going to have the most marvelous time together this summer."

"Wow, that's uh…way nice of your mom, Gretchen, but I've already got plans tonight with Emma."

Emma finally managed to get out from behind Gretchen, positioning herself next to Abby. She smiled brightly, giving Gretchen a dainty little sarcastic wave.

Gretchen—seriously taken aback— gave Emma a once-over, offered a snooty little laugh and replied, "With Emma? Oh… I see." She looked Emma up and down once more for effect. "Well, we will hang out at that little fundraiser thing tonight, won't we? You and I, I mean."

"Ummm…sure, I'll be hanging out with Emma, but you can join us if you'd like."

"Oh," she said, giving Emma another quick, contemptuous up and down, "of course." With that, Gretchen flipped her hair-sprayed head around and strutted off like an indignant princess who was just informed she'd have to mix with the peasants at the royal ball.

Emma and Abby both turned to watch the show Gretchen made of herself as she paraded toward her mother's bright red sports car, parked sideways out in front of the school.

Claudia Buckley, Gretchen's social climbing mother—whose hair was the same unnaturally blinding blonde shade that Gretchen's was—peered impatiently over her larger-than-life sunglasses as her darling daughter came toward the car and climbed into the passenger's seat. Mother and daughter greeted each other with air kisses so as to not mess up Mummy's makeup, then sped off out of sight.

"I think she likes me…no really, she does," Emma said. They both broke into hysterics.

Abby became serious. "I hope you don't mind…even though Gretchen's…well, the way that she is, my mom thinks I should try to be nice to her since she's new in town and doesn't have any friends."

"Gee, I can't possibly imagine why she wouldn't have any, but no worries, I'm totally fine with it."

"Oh, look, your brother's here—with Ozzy! Hey Keith! Hi, Ozzy!" Abby waved enthusiastically toward the rusted out, light blue '57 Chevy truck, which had just pulled up to the curb.

In the driver's seat sat Keith, Emma's sixteen-year-old guitar-plucking, denim-vest-wearing, charming prankster of a brother. His wavy mop of dark brown hair, huge brown eyes and big goofy sideways grin drove almost all the girls in town to distraction—which Emma and Abby could not understand no matter how hard they tried.

Next to him in the passenger's seat was Ozzy, who was not only Keith's inseparable apprentice in mischief but also his pet goat. Ozzy stuck his head out the window, regarding them as he casually chewed on a piece of hay. He was an African pygmy goat, but what he lacked in size, he more than made up for in his personality.

"Hey, Abby, how's it goin'?" Keith waved back; Ozzy continued on with his chewing.

Emma waved back to Keith. "Be there in a minute!"

Keith nodded, then began drumming on the steering wheel. His head bobbed up and down to some tune he was listening to while Ozzy kept time to the beat, bobbing his head up and down as well.

Grabbing their backpacks, the girls headed toward Keith's truck but paused for a moment to take in the display playing out in the front seat.

"They're at it again," said Emma, cracking up.

"I just love that crazy goat," Abby said. "Ever since your brother got his license I've yet to see him cruising around without Ozzy parked next to him."

They watched some more while Keith and Ozzy—both oblivious to their audience—continued on, lost in their own little rock band world.

"Oh yes, they're as thick as thieves. Ozzy's not only his copilot but also his coconspirator—he's been teaching him tricks."

This captured Keith's attention. He stopped his crazed drumming and turned to listen.

"Seriously?" asked Abby.

"Yep, it's true!" Keith smiled, appearing all pleased with himself—which was most often the case.

He also spoke with a slight southern drawl, although they lived nowhere near the south, had never been to the south, or ever knew anyone from there.

"Wow," Abby replied, "I am impressed. It took a goat to do it, but hey, at least someone's been able to teach your brother something."

Both girls snickered while Abby winked at Keith.

"You girls go right ahead and laugh, but Ozzy here's taught me everythin' I need to know, isn't that right, Ozzy…"

Ozzy tipped his head in a knowing nod.

"And I kid you not when I say I've been teachin' my buddy Ozzy here some sweet tricks, and if you're worthy he and I'll put on a show for you sometime."

"Now that should be something," Abby said, amused. Both Emma and Keith were constant sources of amusement for her.

"Oh indeed it will," Keith said, smiling broadly. "You almost ready to go, Emma? Cause Ozzy's gettin' antsy…I promised him some ice cream. You wanna come along with us, Abby?"

"Uh, thanks, Keith, but I'm thinking not. If you recall, the last time I rode with Ozzy he tried to eat my backpack."

Ozzy's expression immediately turned sheepish.

"Hey, don't go blamin' poor Ozzy. He can't help it you left half a PB&J sandwich in there. It beckoned him." He reached over and scruffed up the fur atop Ozzy's head as the goat continued to chew.

"Who's a good goat?" Ozzy contentedly squinted, leaning toward Keith as he totally got into his head rub.

"Actually, I'd love to come but I'm waiting for my mom. She's bringing Cameron back from his chess club."

"Just how is that little monkey of a brother of yours doin' anyway? And shouldn't a puny scrub of a ten-year-old be doin' somethin' more like playing in a sandbox instead of sittin' around beatin' people at chess?"

"The only reason Keith says that," Emma said," is 'cause Cameron put him in checkmate last week. Twice."

"You just wait; I'll beat that little rascal one of these days."

"Sure you will, Keith, you just keep telling yourself that," said his sister, "but for now maybe you oughta just stick to playing in your sandbox."

"Hey, there's nothin' wrong with playin' in a sandbox, is there Ozz-man…"

Ozzy appeared to nod in agreement.

"See? What'd I tell ya?"

Both girls shook their heads and smiled.

Emma threw her backpack into the bed of the truck, opened the passenger's side door and roughed up Ozzy's fur. "Scoot over, you silly goat."

He scooted on command. Emma climbed in and shut the door. The goat nuzzled up next to her as she threw an arm around him, using the free one to wave back at her friend. "See you tonight, Abby!" Abby waved back and watched them leave as Keith's rusted out pride and joy, marked by a license plate that read "Ozzy," coughed and sputtered its way down the street.

Chapter 2

Anticipation filled the air—as well as the smell of bug spray—as the crowd began forming for the fundraiser. The bonfire was ablaze, taking the nip out of the crisp air of an early summer night. An array of twinkling lights was strewn all about the trees, giving a festive, magical glow to the surroundings.

Several tables were piled high with the usual array of party food—meaning every fattening delicacy imaginable—alongside the ever unpopular veggie platters, which no one ever desired to eat from but did so anyway, just so everyone else would think they were health nuts. There was also a makeshift stage set up with balloons and streamers of all colors, and a banner announcing that Ozzmosis would supply the musical entertainment for the evening's Rock the Dock festivities.

All this was in sharp contrast to the state of the beach which gave way to overgrown bushes, downed trees, and knee-high debris scattered everywhere along with a busted up dock sticking haplessly out of the water and a dilapidated shack of a snack bar just to make it complete.

Keith—with Ozzy in tow—made his way through the crowd over to a tree near the stage where he hoped to secure the goat while his band performed.

"Aw, come on, Ozzy, it won't be so bad," Keith said during his futile efforts to tie the indignant goat's leash to a tree.

Ozzy did not appreciate being restrained and had no problem letting Keith know about it as he leapt around like a rodeo horse, attempted to squirm out of his collar several times, and moaned in the manner of a sick, agonized cow giving birth in a field somewhere.

"Do this for me, Ozz-man. I can't have you wanderin' around the fundraiser alone. Last time I gave you free roam at somethin' like this you rammed over an occupied port-a-potty. I doubt that poor man will ever be the same."

Ozzy's eyes twinkled as a look of pride flashed over his face.

"I'm sorry, buddy, but you simply cannot be trusted." Ozzy gave a resigned sigh and allowed Keith to finally get the leash tied.

"Conversing with the goat again?" asked a snide voice from behind him. Keith turned to see Abby's brother, Cameron, smirking at him.

"Hey, you scrappy smidgeon of a scrub, how's it goin'?" Keith said to Cameron who was ten going on thirty-five.

He was a quick-witted, adorable, feisty little elf with light brown hair and twinkly brown eyes, and despite their age differences was in constant cahoots with Keith as they endlessly concocted schemes together.

"Not bad, except I forgot to bring my earplugs to drown out that guitar playing of yours."

"And just what's wrong with my guitar playin'?" Keith asked.

"Nothing, if you enjoy the sound of bees flying into an electric fence."

"Hey, that's not very nice," said Keith, pretending to look offended.

Cameron laughed. "Seriously though, just wanted to wish you good luck tonight."

"Thanks!" said Keith.

"You need me to stay with Ozzy for you?" The goat's ears perked up as he looked eagerly in their direction.

"Nah, go enjoy yourself." Ozzy gave Keith a dirty look. "And keep tabs on just how many chicks are checkin' me out while I'm on stage."

"Hmmm… sounds like a tough order, counting to zero's pretty difficult."

"I'm so gonna get you for that," Keith said, waving a finger in Cameron's general direction.

Cameron swatted it away.

"I'll live in complete fear," Cameron said. Pleased with himself, he gave Keith a mocking smile, turned on his heels and went off to join his sister over by the stage.

A few minutes later as the sun began to set, the bonfire was lit and the townsfolk began to gather around the stage, waiting for the festivities to officially begin.

"Emma, over here!" Abby shouted. Emma just finished helping Keith bring an amplifier up onto stage while the other band members warmed up. She came down to join Abby and Cameron in front of the stage.

"Hey Cameron, how'd the chess meet go?" Emma asked with great enthusiasm.

"You shoulda been there; it was epic!" Cameron beamed. "I destroyed my first opponent in ten minutes flat, then showed no mercy to my second victim who succumbed to checkmate in a mere four moves. I think I need more challenging competition…"

"I remember how badly you beat me the last time we played, and I'm probably still no match for you, but if you want I'd love to give you another game soon," Emma said.

"That'd be great! And I'm sure you'll be far better competition than that pathetic rogue of a brother of yours was last week."

"Oh there's Dad and Uncle Clegg…I think they're about to start," said Abby.

Two men made their way up on to the stage. They looked strangely alike—most likely because they were twins—except 'Uncle Clegg' was as bald as a bowling ball while his brother, Clem, had enough hair for both of them. Clem was never seen without his little round glasses while Clegg was never seen without his trusty coach's whistle. However, they both had the same blue eyes, big dimples and warm friendly smiles.

Abby's dad—Dr. Clem O'Donnell—was a physician, philanthropist, and all-around good guy; his brother Clegg was the coach of the girls' swim team, the athletic coach for the town's high school, mayor of town of Lakewood, and also fit into the category of all-around good guy.

"Wow, what a great crowd!" Clegg said, grabbing the microphone like a bald, middle-aged rock star.

"Welcome to Rock the Dock and thanks for coming out! We're here to celebrate, as our fine town has finally after forty long years, gained access to the lake with this potentially fantastic—but highly neglected—beach and dock. With the funds we're raising tonight, we're going to transform all this into something we can all be proud of for years to come!"

The crowd cheered and clapped.

"That being said, my brother Clem purchased the property and has generously donated it to the town! What's more, our girl's recreational swim team—which I just happen to be the proud coach of—will be able to call this lake home. And now, the man who made all this possible, my brother, Dr. Clem O'Donnell!" Clegg gestured to his brother as the crowd erupted once again into cheers and applause.

Clem nodded humbly and moved toward the microphone.

"Thanks, everyone, but hold your applause for in a few short weeks I'll be applauding you. You've signed up to donate your time and money into making this beach into something our families will enjoy for years to come. And to celebrate this transformation, one month from today, we'll have our very first Fourth of July Lakefront Summer Festival with a lot of good family fun, fireworks, and music from our town's most favorite band."

"And speaking of which, they're here to play for us tonight. So without further ado, I present to you, *Ozzmosis!*"

The crowd went wild as Keith and the other three members quickly ascended onto the stage.

Seizing hold of the microphone, Keith shouted, *"Let's Rock the Dock!"*

More cheers and applause ensued, and almost every girl there—for reasons Abby and Emma could not possibly fathom—went gaga over the geeky lead guitar player in the denim vest, otherwise known as Keith. He grabbed his guitar, flung the strap over his shoulder, and the music began.

A while later, Gretchen and her mom promenaded onto the scene, wearing identical expensive dresses, spike-heels—which they teetered around in, trying in vain to keep their balance in the sand, and enough jewelry between the two of them to fill a pirate's treasure chest to overflowing. They both stuck out in the crowd but certainly not in the way they intended. They made their way over to Abby, Emma and Cameron, who were helping themselves to some goodies from a refreshment table.

"Well hello, Abby! And…of course, Emma," Gretchen said, eyeing Emma with her standard up and down flicker of disapproval.

"We arrived fashionably late as Mummy and I did the whole mother daughter thing at the salon…don't we look fantabulous?" Gretchen threw her arms out in a grand gesture and spun around, displaying what she perceived to be her magnificent wonder.

"Ummm…yeah, you both look great. Right, Emma?" Abby said.

"Huh? Oh, yes, definitely," Emma said as both she and Abby shot each other a quick knowing look.

"Oh, Abby *darling*," Gretchen's mother began, "you and your mom will simply have to get together with Gretch and me and do a whole day, you know, the works: shopping, brunch, the salon? It'll be divine, don't you agree?"

Abby tried hard to keep a straight face as she saw Cameron sneering out of the corner of her eye. "Uh, I guess. I'll have to talk to my mom. We've actually never really been into that whole scene."

She looked toward Emma, who'd turned away to watch her brother making a full-of-himself fool up on the stage.

"Oh, really?" Gretchen's mom said, acting quite surprised. "Well, I would've thought—given your family's position in the community and all—that you'd be accustomed to these things. Of course, I understand if your little friend here…what's your name, dear?"

Only half-listening to the conversation, Emma turned back around. "What? Oh, it's Emma. My name's Emma."

Gretchen's mom gave her the same once over her daughter enjoyed doing. "Oh, that's right, how could I forget? Emma. Such an unassuming name. Well, I could understand if Emma and her mother weren't acclimated to these things as her dad's just a handyman and all," she said in a disdainful tone, "but *your* father's a prominent figure in the community."

"Your mom and you need to start traveling in the right circles." She punctuated this with a small, snooty laugh as her blood-red manicured claws toyed with one of her necklaces.

Abby noticed Emma's eyes were cast downward, and she could tell by her friend's posture that Gretchen's mom was making her uncomfortable. It infuriated her that this woman would behave like such a buffoon to Emma.

Narrowing her eyes, Abby looked at Gretchen's mom in less than a nice manner. "The right circles? I'm not quite sure what you're getting at, Mrs. Buckley, but Emma and her family are the best, and they are definitely the right circles for us."

An indignant look of surprise contorted Mrs. Buckley's face as she opened her mouth to speak, but as if saved by the bell the music stopped, applause broke out, and Keith made an announcement.

"Thanks so much, everyone! The band and I are gonna take a short break, to break into some of those cookies over there before you guys go and snatch 'em all up on us!"

The group of star-struck girls which were gathered at the foot of the stage held on to his every word. Keith made a point to jump down from the stage—hoping the girls would be impressed. They were. It didn't take a lot to impress Keith's fans.

He relieved Ozzy from his outpost at the tree and brought him along to get a snack over to where Emma, Abby, Cameron, Gretchen, and her mom were standing around.

Abby's mom, Elaine, came over and handed Keith a nice big plate of cookies. "Keith, you and the band sound fantastic tonight!" she said.

Elaine O'Donnell was a vibrant, outgoing woman with short, sensible blonde hair and a warm, friendly smile. Tirelessly running pretty much every volunteer committee in the community, she still found time to be a devoted wife and mom. She always wore a strand of pearls, not as a pretentious fashion statement but because they'd belonged to her grandmother, and she and her best friend, Lily— Keith and Emma's mom—were both card carrying members of the Capris Pant Wearing Cookie Bakers Committee.

"Aw shucks, ma'am, it ain't nothin'," Keith said as he gave her a wink and pretended to tip a cowboy hat that wasn't there.

Abby's mom laughed as she turned around and got back work. Emma's eyes rolled at her brother's unending lameness.

"I'm sorry, was that supposed to be music you were playing?" Cameron chimed in. "I thought for sure you guys were trying to imitate the sounds of construction equipment gone bad."

"Gee, thanks a lot, you little vermin." Keith tousled up Cameron's hair and Cameron swatted his hand away, much harder than he had done earlier.

"Hey! Ouch!" Keith said, wringing his hand in mock pain. Ozzy nudged Cameron as if to say good job.

Cameron hugged him as the goat plastered his face with kisses.

"Oh gross! That is repulsive!" Gretchen exclaimed, eyes wide with revulsion. "Abby, your brother's gonna get serious germs from that filthy creature! That, that…*thing* should not be here!"

"I could not agree more!" added Gretchen's mom, looking appalled and arrogant all at the same time.

Ozzy stopped kissing Cameron and took a step in Gretchen's direction.

"Get that thing away from us!" Gretchen continued as she pointed wildly and accusingly toward Ozzy.

Ozzy tilted his head, giving her a curious look.

"Poor Ozzy," Keith said, "you've gone and hurt his feelings."

Ozzy pricked up his ears and swung his head in Keith's direction. Keith subtly gestured toward Gretchen, cuing the goat to perform his latest and greatest trick.

Wasting no time, Ozzy bolted toward Gretchen, jumped on her, then covered her entire face with giant, slobbery kisses. Gretchen screamed and jumped backward, nearly falling off her spiked heels, and pushed Ozzy away from her.

"Help, help, help!!! Oh gross, HELP!!! I've got GOAT GERMS!!! Mummy, HELP!!!" she screeched at the top of her lungs, flapping her arms around like a deranged bird who'd forgotten how to take flight. *"HELP!!!!"*

"Now *that's* funny," Cameron remarked as Gretchen shot him an incredibly evil look.

Abby, Emma, and Keith took it all in, trying their very best to hide their immense enjoyment.

Keith pulled Ozzy back, pretending to scold him, "Now, Ozzy, what have I told you? Shame on you! You need to leave the pretty girls alone…where are your manners?"

Keith continued his charade of innocence. "I speak for both myself and Ozzy when I say we are deeply sorry if he has offended you," he said, patting the goat's head.

Gretchen's mom wasn't buying it.

"You keep that revolting creature away from my daughter, do you hear me, Keith? Your parents will hear about this!"

"Come along, darling," she said to Gretchen, placing an arm around her terror-stricken offspring. "We'll get you straight home and into a nice, hot, bubble bath."

They turned to go, then Gretchen spun back around, "Just so you know, I *DESPISE* that moronic brother of yours, Emma, *and* his disgusting goat. The three of you are nothing but a bunch of riff-raff! And why is your obnoxious brother always wearing that stupid denim vest, anyway? Where'd he find it—in a dumpster?" Whipping her head back around, she and her mother stalked off.

"Hey, just what are you insinuatin' little lady? I'll have you know, I'm quite fond of this here vest!" Keith called out after them, smiling broadly in amusement as he fed Ozzy a cookie.

"I do *not* like that girl," Cameron said, studying them as they wobbled away in their high-heels.

"Neither do I, but your sister has a point in feeling bad for her. And I must admit, as awful as she is, I kinda feel bad for her myself—probably because she *is* so awful—so we gotta at least try to make an effort to be nice, right?"

Emma and Abby exchanged a small smile.

"Hmmmm...I guess, but I still don't like her *or* trust her," Cameron said. "She's trouble."

"Hey, Keith, don't look now, but Gretchen's mom is giving your mom quite an earful." Abby gestured toward the heated monologue taking place at the raffle table his mom was running.

Lily Rhodes—Keith and Emma's mom—was a short, sweet lady, with a great sense of humor and brown, curly shoulder-length hair. A constant sidekick of Elaine O'Donnell, their two families were more like one. She was a stay-at-home mom who loved her family despite the fact that both her son and husband liked to joke about her weight by calling her a butterball. She preferred to think of herself as pleasantly plump.

They watched with great interest as Mrs. Buckley pitched a fit, pointing over and over again in Keith's direction.

"Uh-oh...break's over, GOTTA GO!" With a devious gleam in his big brown eyes, Keith saluted his comrades and broke into a run with Ozzy.

At a lightning speed, he tied Ozzy back to the tree then jumped up onto the stage, motioning wildly to the rest of the band to get the heck back up there and join him. He glanced quickly in his mom's direction and saw her eyeing him with an accusatory look. He smiled sheepishly at her, and the music began. Once again, Keith's entourage of admirers fixed their gaze upon him.

Chapter 3

"What a perfect end to a perfect day," Emma said, sitting next to Abby on the water's edge as they dangled their feet into the lake later that evening.

Farther up the beach what was left of the crowd had gathered around the bonfire, and much to the relief of the ears of every dog in the vicinity, Keith's band had put it to rest for the night.

"Yep, and a great start to summer too!" Abby said, smiling.

She turned to Emma with a look of concern. "I'm really sorry about the ridiculous stuff Gretchen's mom said. That woman was way out of line."

"Oh, don't worry about it" Emma said, trying to brush it off, "she and Gretchen are just really good at showing their true colors."

"You sure?"

"Yep, positive. It's all good." In the darkness Abby couldn't see that her friend's eyes told a different story.

They sat in silence for a moment, staring out at the lake. The moon was full and the sky was decorated with about a billion stars, all reflecting onto the surface of the water.

Emma began to feel more like herself and said, "And those true colors of theirs? I think those would be something like several different shades of puke green with a bit of bright pink added in for effect."

"You truly are demented—do you know that?" Abby teased.

"Why, thank you. I take that as the highest of all compliments," said Emma.

Abby purposefully kicked water at Emma.

"Oh, that's it, it really is!" Emma used both feet to turbo-splash Abby, as Abby shrieked and splashed back.

They both ended up soaked in a fit of laughter.

"We're gonna have such a great time swimming here," Abby said as she splashed Emma again.

"Hey, enough already! And we will, for sure. But just to let you know, I'll win every race our swim team has this summer…while *you* come in last." Emma said, teasing her friend.

"Is that so?"

"Yep, it's so…"

"I'm thinking it'll be the other way around."

"Oh, really? Well, you just keep thinking that…sometimes delusions are far easier to handle than the cold, hard facts of life," Emma said, grinning as Abby splashed her once more.

A serious look suddenly appeared on Abby's face. "Emma, there isn't anything that means more to me than our friendship."

"Not even picking on my brother?"

"Hmmmm…nope. Not even that. Although that is a pretty close second. Remember the time we soaked his hairbrush in green food coloring?"

"That was totally epic," Emma said, and when he saw his hair, his expression was priceless!" They broke into hysterics.

Then Abby turned more serious again. "The reason I brought up our friendship was because I was thinking about Gretchen. If things don't change for her, she may never know what it's like to have a best friend—or any friend for that matter—and that's really sad."

"That *is* sad."

"My mom thinks the reason Gretchen's mom wants she and I to become friends so badly is so they can 'fit in' with the right people—which I guess they've decided we are, in their book. I'll never understand that kind of thinking."

"Sounds like Gretchen's a carbon copy of her mom. She'll never make any real friends that way."

"I know, and that's why we need to find some way to make her see what really matters," Abby said.

"Oh, believe me, I'm *all* for changing Gretchen, but that's one tall order," said Emma. "It might actually be easier to brush an alligator's teeth. But I do think it's awesome of you to wanna help her."

"Like my dad always says, 'If you see someone in need, you've gotta do whatever you can to help them.' If we could show Gretchen what real friendship is like, then who knows—maybe there'd be some hope for her."

"That's a great idea," Emma said. And then a second later a proverbial light bulb went on over her head, "and I've got a great idea of my own…be right back!"

"Hey, where you going?"

Emma scampered up the beach then hurried back a moment later, arriving out of breath carrying an empty bottle, a notepad, pen, and a flashlight.

"What's all this for?"

"We're gonna write a message, stick it in the bottle, then throw it out into the lake," she said, her eyes twinkling as she plopped back down beside Abby.

"How cool! You mean like a message in a bottle?"

"My, you do catch on quick, don't you…" Emma said, never missing the opportunity to pick on her friend.

"What'll we write?"

"About us! Actually, it'll be a wish for whoever finds it. Wishing they're able to find a friendship like ours…you don't think that's lame, do you?"

"Hmmm…well, now that you mention it…" she looked at Emma wickedly, then laughed. "Just kidding. I think it's a brilliant idea."

"Can you hold the flashlight for me?" Abby caught the flashlight Emma tossed in her direction while Emma opened up the notepad and started scribbling away furiously.

Abby rubbernecked, but Emma nudged her away. "Not till it's finished," she ordered. Emma bit away at her lower lip while she continued writing.

"There, done! Let me read it to you…" she said, grabbing the flashlight back. She leapt to her feet and began to read:

This bottle contains the absolute coolest wish for whoever finds it. A wish that you're able to find the kind of friendship I've found with my best friend, Abby. There's nothing better in the whole wide world than a friendship like ours…even though I am a way better swimmer than she is.

Yours Truly,
Emma R.

"It's perfect!" Abby squealed, "except for that last line there."

"What? I see nothing wrong with the truth," she taunted. "Okay, let's roll it up, shove it in the bottle, and let it set sail!"

Emma tore out the page, rolled it up, and handed it to Abby. Then Emma pulled the cork out of the bottle and held it out so Abby could put the message inside. Once she did, Emma went to put the cork in, but of course it refused to cooperate so she had to cram, shove, push with all her might and then finally bang the daylights out of it with the flashlight to get it to at last squeeze down into the bottle.

"Wow that was a lot harder than I thought it would be. Anyway, I think I've got it now. You may have the honors, madam," Emma said, doing the whole fake British accent thing again. "Throw it out into the lake as far as you possibly can."

"It shall be my great pleasure, Lady Emma," Abby replied in her own fake British accent. She whipped the bottle as hard as she could out into the water.

Little did they know that belligerent little cork popped out midair and flew off into the night to explore parts unknown.

"Perfect!" exclaimed Emma.

"It was quite a fine throw if I do say so myself," said Abby.

"Well, we'd better get back up there," Emma said, gesturing up the beach, "before Ozzy comes looking for us…last one back's a loser!" She started running up the beach.

"Hey, no fair! You've got the flashlight!"

Emma stopped and waited for her friend to catch up, "All right, come on, slowpoke."

As soon as Abby reached her, however, Emma took off once more, laughing and leaving her in the dust.

Chapter 4

"**G**o get it, Ozzy!" Keith said as he threw the chewed-up tennis ball across the yard.

Ozzy charged after the ball, grabbed it, then pranced proudly back with it as if he considered himself to be the most amazing goat in all the land.

"Okay, now gimme the ball!" Ozzy blatantly ignored Keith's request, giving him a sly sideways glance as he headed in Cameron's direction.

Keith looked on in betrayed disbelief as Ozzy brought the ball to Cameron.

"Aw, good boy!" Cameron smiled snidely at Keith as he roughed up the tuft of fur atop the goat's head.

"Oh, I see where your loyalties lie now, Ozzy. You just wait till it's time for me to give you some snacks…"

At Keith's words, Ozzy groaned and hung his head down to solemnly contemplate the grass.

It was the day after the fundraiser; Cameron and Abby were next door at Keith and Emma's house—a modest, tidy two-story cape surrounded by a white picket fence, which more or less was usually able to keep Ozzy within its boundaries. Each spring, Emma's mom planted beautiful flowerbeds in the front yard, so beautiful in fact were these flowerbeds that Ozzy thought they looked good enough to eat—and did so each spring for the past five years that he'd been part of their family.

"So when are you gonna show us all these other tricks you've been teaching Ozzy?" Abby asked.

Ozzy raised up his head at this, eagerly looking toward Keith. Just then, Lily came out the back door carrying a tray of cookies and lemonade, setting it down on the patio table. Overhearing the business about Ozzy's tricks, she saw it as the perfect opportunity to discuss the incident Gretchen's mom had been so riled up about.

"Speaking of Ozzy's tricks, Keith, I need to have a little chat with you…"

Keith gulped.

"Gretchen's mom wasn't exactly—how shall I put it— *pleased* with what went down last night." She pointedly raised an eyebrow in his direction and held it there while she awaited his response.

All eyes—including Ozzy's—focused on Keith, and everyone—with the exception of Lily—started snickering.

"Hey, what's everyone lookin' at me for? Ozzy's the one who did it!" Keith said, trying his darnedest to look innocent yet failing miserably.

Ozzy shot Keith a dirty look.

"Ha! I knew it! You made him do that, didn't you!" Emma said, revealing a tone of pride in her voice. Keith smiled, saying nothing.

"Good one!" said Cameron.

"Why, thank you, Cameron," Keith said while he and Cameron, being the nerds that they were, high-fived about it.

"Shame on you, trying to use poor Ozzy as a scapegoat like that," said Abby.

"Baddum-tssss," added Cameron.

"Well, as funny as it all may seem, it wasn't at all amusing to Mrs. Buckley or to Gretchen. Keith, I need you to please refrain from making Ozzy plant any more kisses on that girl—and that's an order," she said, trying to come off as parental as she could while trying to conceal her own amusement.

"Oh, all right…" Keith said. "Ozzy? No more kissing Gretchen, do you hear me?"

Ozzy tilted his head questioningly toward Keith. Lily, knowing fully well her son still had many tricks up his sleeve, contented herself with the fact that if he gave his word not to pull *this* particular prank again, he wouldn't. With that she turned around and started back into the house but suddenly turned back around.

"Oh, by the way, Keith, the mail just came and it would seem you got yet another card from your secret admirer. I put it in your room with the others," she said, then proceeded to go back into the house.

Cameron smirked. "How many letters does that make now?"

"Four in the past two weeks, all from the same person," Emma said.

"How can you be sure they're all from the same person?" Abby asked. "I mean you've seen the way all the girls in town—who apparently have no taste whatsoever—are when it comes to your brother."

Everyone snickered except Keith.

"Hey, they can't help it if they can't resist my charm, talent, and good looks," Keith said.

Ozzy made an exaggerated sound like he coughed something up. Everyone snickered again. Except Keith.

"We know it's the same person because all the cards reek with the same awful smelling perfume," Emma said.

"I wonder who it is?" said Cameron.

"Obviously someone who's not crazy enough to admit publicly that she likes him," Emma said, smiling coyly.

Once again, everyone snickered—except Keith.

"So Keith, how *did* you get Ozzy to do that to Gretchen—I never heard you tell him to get her."

"That's cause Ozzy here," Keith began, "is not only a highly-intelligent creature but also my very well-trained apprentice in mischief. Allow me to demonstrate. Emma? Please stand in front of Ozzy."

With a *what is my idiot brother up to this time* expression, she moved over to face the goat.

"Observe. All I had to say was 'poor Ozzy, you've gone and hurt his feelings.'"

Ozzy spun his head around to look at Keith, and Keith proceeded to make a small gesture toward his sister. The goat sprang into action, pounced on her and covered her whole face in wet, sticky goat kisses.

"Hey! That tickles!" she squealed. Ozzy stopped for a moment to consider her. "Aw, that's okay, Ozzy…I don't mind."

The vigorous licking resumed.

"Okay, okayyyyy…enough! *Enough!*" she said, giggling.

The goat got down. Everyone was in hysterics. Ozzy, satisfied with himself, strode over to Keith for praise and more importantly, a cookie.

"Hmmmm…not bad, what else you got?" Abby said as Emma poured glasses of lemonade for them.

Keith took a sip of his lemonade then put it down. "Okay, we've got time for just one more trick before I've gotta go help Dad pick up some lumber for the dock."

Jack Rhodes was a fun-loving dad and husband, who'd just recently started his own handyman business called 'The Jack of All Trades.' When he chose the name he thought it was hysterical—which said a lot about how lame his sense of humor was—but his family loved him anyway. He and his son looked very much alike except Jack was twenty-five years older and fifty pounds heavier. He was a big teddy bear of a guy who was always more than willing to lend a hand. Hence, why he became a handyman.

Keith pointed over to his dad, who'd just emerged from the basement's bulkhead carrying a tool bag big enough to store a family of five.

After his dad walked past and was heading toward the driveway, Keith got a crafty look on his face and whispered, "Get a load of this…" Then in a regular voice, "Hey, Ozzman."

Ozzy instantly turned to face Keith.

"Dad is such a klutz," he said, pointing toward his father.

Ozzy looked at Keith's dad, then back at Keith, and to his dad once more. Displaying what could only be described as a completely devious grin, Ozzy charged full-speed at Keith's dad, ramming him as hard as he could and nearly knocking him right over as the tool bag went flying. The goat was quite pleased with himself. Everyone started laughing.

"Keith?!?!" His dad said, smiling in good humor as he turned around to pat Ozzy and eye his son.

"I'll never understand why everyone always blames me for this stuff…" Keith said, looking every bit as guilty as he was.

"Okay, prankster," his dad said, "I'm ready to go to the lumberyard whenever you are…but Ozzy stays here."

Ozzy looked back and forth between Keith and his dad, desperately pleading with his eyes to be taken along.

"Aw come on… look at him, Dad! He wants to go!"

"No way. Last time we brought him there he ate a pile of woodchips, half a small tree, and part of a pallet. The goat stays. Sorry, Ozzy."

Sighing in hopeless despair, Ozzy walked over to Keith and pressed his head up against him for solace.

Keith looked down at the forlorn goat. "Poor Ozzy…you heard what the evil ogre said, you gotta stay home." He patted Ozzy, trying to offer him some small reassuring comfort.

"Dad, you do realize that Ozzy may very well need therapy for this kind of rejection…?"

Keith's dad smiled, shook his head, picked up the bigger than life tool bag and headed toward his truck.

"Bye, Dad, see ya, Keith. I'll look after Ozzy for you!" Emma said, waving.

Ozzy trudged over to the patio table and dejectedly plopped himself down.

"So, I'm up for that chess game now, Emma. That is, *if* you dare…" Cameron said, his eyes gleaming.

"You're on, kiddo. Let's go set up a game. Come on Ozzy, you can watch."

Begrudgingly, Ozzy got up followed along behind Emma and Cameron.

"You coming, Abby?" Emma said as she noticed Abby lagging behind.

"I can't…I totally forgot Gretchen and her mom are dropping by to have a look at our pool because they're putting one in at their new house and are looking for ideas for theirs. Mom thought I should be there," Abby said, looking less than thrilled at the prospect. "I don't suppose you wanna come along?"

"Ah, no. I'd much rather just let your brother destroy me at chess if you don't mind. That *is* your plan, isn't it, Cameron? To destroy me at chess?"

"Painfully destroy you, actually," Cameron said brightly.

"I'd also rather be attacked by rabid wolves than have another dose of the Buckleys right now, thank you very much. So yeah, I'm good. I'll just stay here."

"I couldn't agree more," Cameron added, "pretty much anything's better than spending time with Wretched Gretchen."

Emma raises her eyebrows at this, then she and Cameron both laughed heartily.

"Wretched Gretchen, I like it," said Emma, smiling wickedly.

"Thanks."

"Cameron, that's really not very nice," Abby said, trying to keep a straight face.

"Hey, blame Keith…" Cameron said.

"Did he call her that?" asked Emma, wondering if she'd have to stoop to feeling sisterly pride twice in one day.

"Nah, I just think it's fun to see Keith get blamed for stuff."

All three of them cracked up at this. Even Ozzy looked amused.

"Seriously guys, we gotta make an effort to be nice to her. I really think she has no clue how she comes across to people…"

"Neither do rabid wolves, but that doesn't mean we need to cozy up to them and give them a hug," Cameron added.

His sister shot him a look. "Cameron?"

"What?" Cameron said, feigning innocence.

"You know exactly what," she said, eyeing him.

Abby looked down the street from the Rhodes side lawn and sighed heavily—despite her self-professed efforts to sound nice about Gretchen—as she watched Gretchen and her mom climb out of their sports car, simultaneously fluffing up their hair and smoothing down their matching outfits.

"Oh boy…I'd better get going," Abby said.

"All righty then, have fun," Emma imparted to her friend.

"See ya later. Sure you don't wanna come along, Emma?"

"Very sure," she smiled wryly, turning to go into the house but then quickly turned back around again. "Oh, Abby, I almost forgot…I've got something for you! Hold on!"

Emma dashed into the house. Seconds later she came out carrying a small wrapped package. "For you," she said, handing it to Abby.

"Wow, thanks! What's it for?"

"It's a birthday present."

"But my birthday's not for another week," Abby said.

"Doesn't matter…open it!" Emma said, beaming.

Excitedly, Abby ripped off the paper in two seconds flat to reveal a journal with an image of a moonlit lake on the cover.

"Emma, it's perfect…thank you! The lake on the journal looks just like our lake did last night!" Abby said, running her hand over the cover.

"Yeah, I know. That's why I gave it to you today. I thought it was kind of a cool coincidence. I got it weeks ago—actually I got myself one as well—they're both the same. You always said you wanted one, and now we can both have one so we can write about all the adventures we have together."

"That's such a cool idea…thank you so much! Can't wait to start writing in it." Abby reached over and gave Emma a quick hug, and much to Ozzy's great delight ended up dropping the wrapping paper in the process.

Ozzy nabbed it, took off with it, then ripped it to shreds all over the yard.

"I've really got to go now or Mom's gonna kill me. Thanks again, see you guys later!" Abby turned and made tracks toward her house.

"By the way, don't forget to tell Gretchen that I'm just *so sorry* I missed her," Cameron sarcastically called out after her.

"Be nice, Cameron…" his sister shot back.

Emma and Cameron watched in deep pity as Abby made her way home to meet up with Mrs. Snotbags and her unpleasant little spawn.

Chapter 5

"**W**elcome to the first day of swim practice at the lake!" announced Clegg as the girls' swim team erupted into cheers and applause.

There were a few passing clouds in the sky with a threat of rain much later on, but other than that it was a warm, beautiful sunny day. Perfect weather for a swim in the lake.

Emma's dad and Keith were busy laying new planks of wood on the dock, and Ozzy—never far from Keith's side—was unhappily tied to a tree once again but hadn't put up nearly the stink he'd done before at the fundraiser, as this time Keith did what any rational goat owner would do in such a situation and bribed him with junk food.

"Just three things I wanna make clear," Clegg said to the team. "First, be careful around the main dock ...lotta nails and loose boards there. Second, do not—I repeat, *do not*—swim on the far side of the floating dock or use the diving board since it's aimed in the same direction. There's a massive amount of thick, tangled weeds growing over there and someone could easily get tangled up. So steer clear; it's *very* dangerous. Did everyone hear that?"

They all nodded like a row of obedient little bobble-head dolls.

"We'll see what can be done about it soon, and we'll move the diving board to the other side next week. And, third, if you see Ozzy in the water tell him to get out… he's only the mascot, not a member of the team. Besides, he needs water wings…"

Some of the girls giggled while Ozzy looked up from work of chewing the grass, squinted bitterly and groaned.

"Actually, my brother's the one who needs water wings," added Emma.

Laughter broke out all around. A sinister-looking smile even seemed to makes its way across the goat's face.

Keith pointedly pointed a level in his sister's direction. "Hey, Pipsqueak, I heard that!"

Emma shot her brother a victorious look. She was also pacing excitedly back and forth while all the other girls were sitting in the sand as she was having a very hard time containing her enthusiasm about finally getting to swim in the lake.

"Okay, girls…after a small warmup, we'll do some races. Just please keep in mind what I said about those weeds," Clegg told them.

The team—which consisted of a dozen girls from ages ten to fourteen—got up, put down their backpacks, towels and other essentials girls that age carry around with them and headed down toward the water.

Gretchen strolled up behind Emma and tapped her on the shoulder. "Well, Emma, it's really too bad we can't use the diving board here just yet, isn't it? And it must be especially disappointing for you," she said, contorting her face into an expression of cattiness.

A bit confused and more than slightly annoyed, Emma said, "Why would it be *especially disappointing* for me?"

"Hmmm…well, maybe I shouldn't have said anything…"

Emma sighed. "Gretchen, if you have something to say, just spit it out."

"Well," Gretchen began, obviously enjoying herself, "there's been…*talk*…that your dives could use…*a bit of work.*"

"Oh, really?" Emma said, folding her arms while suspiciously fixating her eyes on Gretchen.

"I'm afraid so but, oh dear, I've really gone and said too much. I think that perhaps when Abby confided in me she was only feeling concerned for you."

"Abby?" You're saying Abby told you this?" Emma gave an incredulous laugh. "I'm sorry, Gretchen, but I don't believe you."

"I am quite sorry for mentioning it. Why, I'm certain Abby wouldn't want you to feel bad about yourself. I think she was just concerned that you might—how shall I put it— embarrass yourself—or maybe even the whole team. Anyway, please don't tell her that you know—I'd simply hate to see the two of you at odds with each other."

Emma narrowed her eyes, giving Gretchen a look of disgust, turned around and continued down toward the lake. She knew Gretchen was a despicable creature but had never been more keenly aware of it than at that very moment. She stopped suddenly and stood still as a couple of things came to mind which made her wonder if maybe there was some truth in what Gretchen said.

A week before school got out, she'd attempted a difficult dive at Abby's pool, which she bombed miserably. Emma remembered Abby's relentless teasing about it. Then at the town pool while Emma was trying out a different dive she lost her balance, producing a highly undignified plop into the water. She seemed to recall the whole team getting a great kick out of it.

Gretchen came up behind her a second time. "Emma? Emma! You look a thousand miles away. No hard feelings, k?"

Emma whipped around and glared at her. In return Gretchen—pleased as punch—smiled winningly and went on her merry way down into the water. Emma eyed her intensely, contemplating the idea of Gretchen getting carried off by some mysterious swamp creature that lurked in the deep, dark depths of the lake.

"Hey, you ready to get in or what?" Abby said, interrupting Emma's detailed imaginings.

Emma turned around, pointedly looked Abby straight in the eyes, and asked, "Do my dives stink?"

"Your dives? Oh, you mean that strange way you have of getting yourself into the water?" she teased.

Teasing each other was just what they always did—only in this instance Emma seemed to take it seriously, looking visibly upset.

"Hey, I'm sorry. I was only joking. You, Emma Rhodes, are an *amazing* diver."

Emma looked up, not even remotely convinced, "Amazing?"

"Of course. Seriously, you're great at diving," Abby said, wondering why her friend would doubt it. "What's wrong?"

"Nothing," she said, shaking her head, appearing to snap out of it as she put on a big smile. "I'm just being stupid. Last one in's a rotten egg!"

"Hey!" said Abby and took off running after her friend. After a few minutes of swimming, splashing and other assorted mayhem, Clegg blew his whistle—his trusty whistle, which he curiously never left home without. He'd made his way out to the floating dock in an old rowboat they'd found buried under some brush. It appeared to be in slightly rough but usable condition, which would come in handy for him as for some strange reason even though he was a swim coach he was very rarely ever seen in the water.

"Okay, get ready girls, this will be our first officially unofficial race of the season. Climb up and get in position."

The girls climbed up onto the floating dock and lined up along the edge.

Clegg held out his stopwatch. "Really simple," he said, "to the shore and back... Ready? Set? Go!"

All of the girls dove effortlessly into the water—with the exception of Emma who slipped and made an awkward, self-conscious kerplunk into the water.

"Careful with your footing there, Emma. You okay?" Clegg asked.

Emma nodded disgruntledly and took off swimming. Her blunder didn't affect her speed, however, as she was soon neck and neck with another girl who'd been in the lead. That girl happened to be Gretchen.

Noticing Emma beside her she shouted out, "See what I mean about your dives?"

After another few seconds, Gretchen deliberately shoved into Emma and tried to push past her. Emma looked daggers at her, then shot out in front of her royal wretchedness, leaving her far behind and making it back to the dock before anyone else.

"And it's Emma in first place!" Clegg called out. "Great job, Emma!"

"Thanks, Coach!" Emma said, thrilled that after such a horrible start she'd win the very first practice race at the lake.

Everyone else quickly finished and cheered her on—all except Gretchen whose facial expression took on the look of someone who'd just downed a jalapeno and lemon sandwich.

Shortly afterward, they had another race with Emma easily taking the lead and coming in first once again.

"Keep this up, Emma, and you'll be taking home a medal for that big race we're having on the Fourth of July!" Clegg said.

"Not if I have anything to do with it," Abby said, smiling.

"Oh, is that what you think? Keep dreaming, O' Donnell!" Emma said, giving her a sly grin as they both began to splash each other—because, of course, they weren't wet already from swimming.

Still seething, Gretchen displayed yet another one of her award winning nasty looks—her green eyes sparking into flames—as jealously continued to consume her.

Once everyone was back up on shore and toweling off, Clegg addressed them once again. "Great practice today, girls! I'm seeing some really strong swimming from all of you. I'll be out of town the rest of the week, so our next practice won't be until Monday. But weather permitting, after that, we'll practice every weekday throughout the summer. Same time, same place. So I'll see you all next week!"

Everyone got dressed, collected up their stuff, and said their goodbyes. Abby went over to talk to Emma's dad. Gretchen started to walk past Emma but couldn't resist taking one last jab. "Too bad you can't dive nearly as well as you can swim."

Emma squinted in her direction, pretending to ignore the remark. "You know, I can't believe you shoved into me and tried to cut me off...are you so desperate that you think the only way to beat me is by pulling something sleazy?"

"Shove into you? *Try to cut you off?*" Oh, Emma, don't be so silly. I would never even dream of doing such a thing," she said, punctuating her words with a weird little giggle.

"Hmmm, now where is Abby? Ah yes, there she is." Gretchen's expression turned from malicious to amiable in a millisecond, then made a huge to-do of waving to Abby. "See you later, Abby! I'll give you a call tonight!"

Abby, looking a bit surprised, waved back. Emma watched the exchange, marveling at how two-faced Gretchen really was. Gretchen took the opportunity to turn around and give Emma another snide look before she departed.

The beautiful blue sky they'd had all morning was quickly becoming ominously overcast, and the temperature was dropping rapidly. Emma compared the sudden change in weather with the effect Gretchen had on everything, everywhere she went. Emma glanced over at Abby, who was thoroughly engrossed in something over on the dock.

"Hey, Abby…you coming back in the water or what?"

"What are you, crazy? It's getting cold…plus, your dad's gonna teach me how to use a power drill! Get dressed and get up here, he could teach both of us!" Abby said.

"Not today. I just wanna swim a while longer before the storm hits. You sure you don't wanna get back in the water?"

"Yeah, I'm sure. Hey, Keith, I think Emma's part fish!"

"Nah, she's *all* fish; my parents adopted her when she was just a guppy," Keith said, cracking himself up with his sad attempt at being funny.

"Of all the brother's in the world, why did I get stuck with the lamest one of them all?" Emma said.

Keith pulled a mock sad face, and Emma grinned.

"Don't go out too deep, kiddo…and stay where we can see you," Emma's dad said.

"Yes, Dad," Emma sighed, rolling her eyes.

Emma's dad turned back around and proceeded to teach Abby all the highly fascinating facts pertaining to the use of a power drill.

Not understanding what the possible lure of that could be, Emma shook her head. She started swimming back and forth in a small area near the dock while she watched everyone else, all busy with what they were doing up on the dock. Ozzy regarded her from his post on the beach while he chewed yet another mouthful of grass.

Her mind flooded with thoughts of what Gretchen told her Abby had said about her dives. *Abby really wouldn't have said that, would she?* Emma wondered. She also thought of how she'd lost her footing today before the first race, which morphed into the memory of screwing up her dive at Abby's house, which gave way to how the team had laughed themselves silly when she colossally lost her balance at the town pool.

Emma looked over at the diving board on the far side of the floating dock, then looked back at the group working on the dock—who were very much wrapped up in their work, the sound of the power drill blaring away and drowning out their words. She looked determinedly back at the diving board then made her decision; she'd just practice a couple dives before anyone was the wiser.

Chapter 6

"I know they're not exactly high fashion, but you'll need to wear these safety glasses at all times," Emma's dad instructed Abby. "You never know when a stray nail, screw or piece of wood could fly up and hit you in the eye. Accidents can happen when you least expect them."

Crouching on the dock next to Emma's dad, Abby put on the ridiculously ugly safety glasses and imagined how thoroughly Emma was going to enjoy making fun of her for wearing them. She turned around to take a quick look out into the water to see if Emma already was laughing at her, except Abby didn't see her.

Abby stood up and took off the glasses to get a better look around. Still no sight of her. She figured maybe Emma had gone back to shore since it was getting so cold, but there was no sign of her there, either. She took one more scan of the lake and froze. Abby spotted a disturbance in the water on the other side of the floating dock where the thick, tangled weeds were.

Panic set in. "Emma?" she said, barely above a whisper at first, hoping beyond all hope that Emma wasn't where she thought she was. Then she began to scream, "EMMA? *EMMA?!?!*"

"Abby, what's wrong?" Jack immediately shot up, alarmed at the visible terror in Abby's eyes as she pointed in the direction of the floating dock. He quickly turned to look.

"I think she's over there, stuck in the weeds!" Abby shrieked.

"Oh dear God," he said, now seeing the disturbance in the water for himself. By this time Keith and Clegg saw it too.

"EMMA?!?!" Abby screamed again.

"Everyone in the boat, *NOW!*" yelled Jack.

"I'll get there faster if I swim," Clegg said, diving in.

In less than a second, Jack and Abby jumped into the rowboat as Keith untied it from the dock and swiftly jumped in after them. The storm clouds overhead gave way to a burst of rain as the wind started to pick up, making the previously calm waters of the lake choppy. Jack rowed strong, quick strokes while Keith and Abby called out Emma's name over and over again, hoping for a response. In less than a minute they reached the floating dock.

Clegg surfaced in front of them. "She's stuck in the weeds and struggling to get out!" he yelled.

"Abby, call 911—NOW!" Jack ordered, tossing her his phone.

Clegg disappeared back down into the water as Jack leapt in after him. Abby was about to follow them, but Keith grabbed her arm.

"Abby, no! It's too dangerous!"

"But I wanna help her!" she said, trying to pull away.

"No! Please, you gotta stay put and call for help!"

She nodded and started to cry. Keith let go of her, quickly tied off the boat and plunged in himself.

Abby held the phone and began to dial 911, but noticed—to her utmost horror—that the phone's screen was blank. "NO! YOU HAVE GOT TO BE KIDDING ME!" Abby screamed furiously as her trembling fingers kept trying to turn it on, hoping beyond all hope it was just switched off. It wasn't—the phone was dead. She threw it across the boat in frustration.

With tears streaming down her face, she jumped up onto the dock and ran across to the side where the disturbance had been. Abby paced anxiously back and forth in the downpour, peering down into the depths that revealed nothing. She kept vigil over the surface of the water as she prayed in absolute desperation.

By the time Jack and Keith made it down to Emma, she'd stopped struggling and was now eerily floating upright. Straightaway, Jack began working with Clegg to try and free her, but panic tore through Keith when he saw Emma like that; he shot up out of the water to breathe.

"What's happening? WHERE'S EMMA?" Abby shrieked as Keith gasped for air.

"She's still stuck, but we're gonna get her out!" was all he could bring himself to tell her. "Stay here!" With that, Keith disappeared back down into the water.

"NO! KEITH, WAIT!!! I NEED YOUR PHONE! KEITH!" she screamed helplessly after him, but he couldn't hear her.

Seconds felt like years as Clegg, Jack, and Keith worked frantically to get her out but it seemed an impossible situation. To make matters worse, when she'd struggled to break free Emma had become even more entangled.

Jack stopped as if remembering something and quickly reached into his pocket. He pulled out a Swiss army knife and instantly began to cut away at the thick weeds ensnaring his daughter's legs.

Suddenly Jack and Clegg resurfaced, carrying Emma— her body limp and lifeless in their arms. Abby watched, frozen in terror—unable to move or speak. Keith scrambled up onto the dock to help them hoist her up. They gently placed her on her back, the rain pelting down on her mercilessly as she laid there. Clegg quickly evaluated the situation.

"She's not breathing!" Clegg yelled. Immediately, he tipped Emma's head back and began mouth-to-mouth resuscitation.

"Dear God, no!" Jack sighed heavily, then anxiously looked toward shore. "How long before they get here?" he said, turning toward Abby.

She said nothing, her eyes huge and fixed on Abby.

"ABBY!" he said with far greater urgency. "Did they say how long it'd be?"

This broke her out of her trance. "I COULDN'T CALL THEM—YOUR PHONE WAS DEAD!" She began to cry hysterically.

"I'll use mine!" Keith said. He grabbed his phone out of his vest pocket, but it was no use—his phone was soaked.

"It's not workin'! Clegg, gimme yours!" Keith yelled.

"It's in my truck. Keys are back on the dock!" He quickly got out, then continued with the mouth-to mouth.
 Without hesitation, Keith plunged into the choppy water of the lake and swam hard for shore. A moment later Emma regained consciousness and violently began coughing up water. Abby scrambled over and knelt down next to her while Clegg and Jack turned Emma onto her side.

"Thank God," Jack said, reaching out to cradle his daughter, holding her head up and pushing wet tendrils of hair back away from her face.

"Emma!!! You're okay!!!" Abby cried out.

Jack kept holding Emma in his arms while she continued to cough. Suddenly she stopped coughing and went limp again. "Emma? Emma?!?! *Wake Up!*"

"*NO!*" Abby wailed.

"She's unconscious." Clegg said. "We've got to get her into that boat and back to shore."

Clegg helped Jack gently, but swiftly, lift her into the boat as Abby jumped in behind them. Clegg untied the boat, then rowed them back as fast as he could while the rain relentlessly continued to pour down upon them. Once they were halfway back across the lake they could see the ambulance pulling down onto the beach.

By the time the boat got to shore the medics were already waiting at the water's edge. They wasted no time reaching into the boat, carefully taking Emma from her dad's arms in the driving rain and placing her on the stretcher. They strapped her in and quickly took her vitals while Jack, Keith, Clegg, and Abby looked on anxiously.

"I called Mom. She's gonna meet us at the hospital," Keith said.

His father nodded, putting an arm around his son's shoulders. The medics lifted Emma's stretcher into the back of the ambulance.

"I'm her father, and this is her brother. We're coming with you."

"Of course, get in," said one of the medics. Keith and his dad climbed into the back of the ambulance.

"We'll meet you at the hospital," Clegg called to them.

The medics quickly shut the back doors of the ambulance. The siren came on, and in less than an instant they were on their way to the hospital.

Chapter 7

The emergency room doors of Lakewood Hospital flew open as the team of medics rushed Emma in on the stretcher through a seemingly endless expanse of hallway, with her dad and Keith hurrying alongside them.

"We need a doctor here, *stat!* This patient is *not* responding!" yelled one of the medics to the admitting nurse.

"Dr. O'Donnell's already on his way," said the admitting nurse standing behind the desk.

Another nurse appeared, carrying a clipboard. "What's going on?" she said, hurrying along beside them.

"Near drowning incident. She'd stopped breathing and was resuscitated at the scene, but she's lost consciousness again, and her limbs are becoming cold and mottled," the head medic told her.

"Vitals?"

"Very shallow breathing, pulse is thirty-eight, blood pressure's fifty over thirty and dropping.

"Get her into room two, *NOW!*" the clipboard nurse ordered.

The medics sped Emma toward the first room on the right as yet another nurse was there holding open the doors. They began to turn the corner into the room with Jack and

Keith following alongside, but the nurse held her arm out in front of them.

"I'm sorry, but you'll both have to wait out here," she said in a clinically cold, yet sympathetic, tone.

Jack reached out quickly, grabbing onto his daughter's cold hand and squeezing it. "Emma, we'll be right out here," he said, looking down at his unconscious daughter's pale, innocent face.

He let go of her hand as they wheeled her into the room, the swinging door abruptly shutting in front of them.

Keith and his dad stood side by side feeling powerless while they watched through the window as the medical team began to work on Emma.

Another nurse called out as a doctor emerged quickly from the elevator, "Dr. O' Donnell, room two!"

The doctor hurried toward the room, instantly recognizing his next door neighbors standing outside the room.

"Jack? What's happened?" he asked as he looked back and forth between Keith and his dad.

"Clem, it's Emma, she's unconscious. She nearly drowned at the lake," Jack managed to get out.

"God, no. I am so sorry. Okay, let me get in there. Be strong and we'll keep you posted." Clem grasped Keith's shoulder and tried to give him a reassuring look as he dashed into the room.

"She *is* gonna be all right Dad, isn't she?" said Keith, his voice cracking, looking far more like a little boy in this instance than the confident sixteen-year-old he was.

Jack reached out and hugged his son. "We gotta have faith, Keith, okay? And we gotta be strong for Mom when she gets here."

Keith nodded and his dad patted him on the back. They continued to watch through the window as Dr. Clem O'Donnell, the man who'd been more like a family member than a neighbor for the past fourteen years—and who was as fond of Emma as he was of his own daughter, Abby—took charge.

"Jack, Keith!" Clegg called out as he and Abby hurried toward them from the ER entrance.

"Please tell me she's doing better. She is, isn't she?" Abby said. They hesitated while her eyes searched theirs for the answers she hoped to find.

"Abby, your dad's in there with Emma," Clegg said. She turned in the direction of the window. "He'll do everything he possibly can for her," he added, trying to reassure her.

The color instantly drained from Abby's face as a wave of reality crashed down upon her. She spotted Emma lying motionless as the urgency of the medical staff gave away the answers Jack and Keith couldn't.

"No," she said barely above a whisper as tears began to flow.

"Let's go sit down," Clegg said, putting his arm around Abby's shoulder, guiding his niece away from the window.

Just then Emma's mom came running down the corridor, followed by Abby's mom and Cameron, who hung back at a slight distance to give Emma's family a bit of privacy.

"Where is she? Where's my little girl?" cried Lily.

Her husband and son turned instantly to the sound of her voice; they both moved quickly toward her and hugged her tight.

"She's in there," Jack said, pulling back and gesturing toward the room.

She quickly headed for the door, but her husband caught her by the arm. "We can't go in, Lily. They want us to wait out here for right now."

She looked back at him in disbelief, then through the window and gasped. She raised quivering hands up to cover her mouth as she saw the body of her lifeless daughter hooked up to countless medical machines. Her husband put his arms around her in an attempt to provide comfort in a circumstance where no such thing existed.

"Oh dear God, please let her be okay," she said.

Abby, noticing her mom and her brother standing a short distance away, got up from her seat and hurried over to them.

"Dad's in there with her. Oh, Mom, please tell me she's gonna be okay, *please!*" Abby begged.

"She has to be okay!" Cameron said.

Elaine reached out, holding on to both of her children tightly. "She really needs our prayers right now. But you know what? Your dad's the best doctor there is, and between him doing everything medically possible for her and God's looking out for her, she's in the best of hands. Everything's going to be all right," she said, wishing she felt as confident as she sounded.

Abby quickly pulled away. *"This is all my fault!"*

"Oh, Abby…sweetheart, of course it isn't your fault," her mom said, trying to hug her again, but Abby was inconsolable.

She turned to face the direction of Emma's room, anger flaring in her eyes. "I should've been there with her, Mom! If I had been, then none of this would be happening."

Her mom stepped forward, tenderly putting her hands on Abby's shoulders, but Abby pushed it away.

"We made a pact, and I didn't hold up my end of it," Abby said, her anger forming tears in her eyes.

"What pact?" Cameron said, coming over to them.

"Last week, right after school got out, we made a pact to be inseparable for the entire summer. She asked me twice to go back in the water with her and I didn't. This is all my fault!"

Just then a nurse flung open the door to ER Room 2. *"CODE BLUE! CODE BLUE! PATIENT'S GONE INTO CARDIAC ARREST!"*

Everything after that happened with lightning speed, yet appeared as if in dreamlike slow motion, illuminated by the uncaring glare of the hospital's fluorescent lights. Emma's mom appeared to cry out, yet no sound was heard as her knees buckled beneath her. Her husband and Keith caught her just in time, supporting her from falling. The three of them huddled together as several more members of the medical staff charged down the hall and in through the doors of Emma's room. One of the nurses drew the curtains on the other side of the window to block the view.

Abby stood frozen as she watched the devastating scene unfold before her. "Mom? What exactly do they mean by cardiac arrest?"

Elaine put her arms around her children, eyes closed in silent, pleading prayer.

"What does it mean, Mom?!?" Abby said, demanding a response, her eyes fixated on Emma's family's reaction.

Elaine hesitated, desperately wanting to shield her children—especially her daughter, who was Emma's best friend—from the truth.

"Mom?"

"…It means her heart's not beating," her mom finally said.

"No!" Abby cried out, *"NO!"*

Chapter 8

"CODE BLUE! CODE BLUE! PATIENT'S GONE INTO CARDIAC ARREST!"
From what seemed like a surreal, distant dream Emma heard these words, murmured and fuzzy, as if she were still underwater and they were being spoken from above the surface.

Suddenly, she experienced a strange but wonderful sensation of weightlessness as she began to feel herself rise up above the bed. As if this wasn't weird enough, she looked down beneath her and saw that she—or at least her body—was still on the bed as Clem and several others frantically working on her. From the gist of what they were saying, she determined they were trying to get a pulse and bring her back.

Not afraid in the least, Emma was more than a bit confused as to what was going on. Why did they think they'd lost her when clearly she was fine? She tried to convey that to them, but they had no clue she was even there. Was she dreaming? How could she possibly be hovering up above everyone while she could see her body lying on a bed? Yet she was. Despite how questionably bizarre it all was, Emma was filled with great tranquility.

Her senses were heightened as never before. Colors took on indescribable depth, beauty, and vibrancy. She was surrounded by the smell of fresh roses even though there were none to be seen, and she could faintly hear what sounded like the voices of a thousand angels singing in the distance. She felt the energy and the emotions of the people in the frenzied scene below—a mixture of both hope and despair—all of them desperate to save her. But save her from what?

After traveling through the wall of the room as if it were nothing more than a sheet of mist, she observed her family, Clegg, Abby, Cameron, and their mom just outside of a room marked ER 1. She sensed the heartbreak and devastation each and every one of them felt. Her mom sobbing uncontrollably while her dad and Keith held her to keep her on her feet; she felt her mom's pain and knew that it was the worst pain anyone could ever feel. She saw the horror on Abby's face and was aware of her overwhelming sorrow. Her brother—always the joker, relentlessly teasing and tormenting her—was crushed beyond all reason. Even though Emma felt the intensity of all their emotions, she still maintained a sense of peace.

Tall luminous figures with long flowing hair, dressed in dazzling white garments, stood beside each of her loved ones reaching out to comfort them, yet she was the only one aware of their presence. Emma tried her hardest to tell them there was no need to be sad, but they couldn't hear her.

Having no real control over where she went, Emma was effortlessly brought through the outside wall of the hospital. Her new view encompassed the parking lot, where Ozzy paced nervously back and forth in the front seat of Clegg's truck.

Abruptly, he stopped pacing and peered out the window, looking directly up at Emma. He could see her! She felt his great sadness turn to joy.

"Hi, Ozzy!" she said as he tilted his head to the side.

How could he see her when no one else could? She sensed his calmness now and knew that on some level he understood what was happening, even though she wasn't completely sure of what it was herself.

Ozzy continued to watch her as she started floating up, higher and higher, very slowly at first—like a poof of smoke gently winding through a chimney, moving farther and farther from away from the parking lot.

Then, out of nowhere, as if she were being whisked away in a turbo-charged vacuum, the world below disappeared from Emma's view. She'd been to more than a few amusement parks in her life, but their most exhilarating rides had nothing on this.

Looking up, she saw she was traveling in what appeared to be a swirling tunnel, its walls constructed solely of soft, white light. At the end of tunnel was the most magnificent, intensely beautiful, warm glowing light she'd ever experienced. Emma was being physically drawn into this light and realized that not only did it radiate perfect peace, love and beauty, it *was* perfect peace, love and beauty. Never had she felt such an awareness of anything in her life. She also knew she was safe from all harm.

The light both enveloped her and filled her. Emma felt she'd known this light her entire life and that it had known her much longer than that. She was also aware that it was more than just light; it was a being, but more than a being— it was the very essence of being itself. Emma felt with great certainty that she was in the presence of God. Time stood still as she drank in the intoxicating splendor of it all.

God spoke to her. Emma could clearly understand everything He said, yet heard nothing. He spoke to her very soul.

She was being given a choice. She could stay here and spend all of eternity in a pure state of happiness—where there was no pain or suffering or sadness—or she could return to her family and loved ones. He also told her that if she were to return to her family and friends she too would suffer pain—not a whole lot different than the pain the people she loved were experiencing right now.

Emma had never felt so torn. She didn't want to leave; nothing could compare to this. This fulfilled her soul more than anything she had experienced in her past. However, she felt it would be completely selfish to stay here when it would cause so much grief for the people she cared about. Maybe this was her chance to help people—those people she loved so very much—by taking away their sorrow, even though she would have to embrace suffering herself as a consequence.

It was settled. She knew her desire to ease their pain was far greater than her desire to be free from it. He reminded her if she went back she'd go through a very difficult trial and would reach a point where she wished she'd stayed but that in the end love and truth would conquer all.

The perfect clarity she felt told her going back was the right decision. He confirmed to her she'd made the right choice. However, He warned her a third time that she would suffer. She said she was willing to do whatever it took to take away their suffering.

God then revealed she would not remember their conversation about the suffering she'd face, only that she'd been given a choice. She held firm in her convictions and knew for certain that someday she would be here again but that now was not her time.

Suddenly Emma felt the sensation of falling, not unlike the feeling of diving off the high board but about a billion times faster.

"WE'VE GOT A PULSE!"

Chapter 9

Time stood still as the seconds on the clock outside ER room 1 deafeningly ticked by, one by one. The medical staff continued to work on Emma behind closed doors and pulled curtains. Each beat of the second hand seared through Lily Rhodes as a reminder that her daughter's heart should also be beating but wasn't.

It had been nearly ten long minutes since the nurse announced Emma was in cardiac arrest. Those words hung in the air like a heavy iron cloud, bearing down on all of them. Not a word was spoken as they all silently prayed for Emma.

The door to ER room 1 swung open. It startled Emma's mom, making her jump. Her husband quickly put his arm around her as they braced for the worst.

However, Clem emerged smiling broadly. "We've got a pulse!"

Immense relief flooded over everyone who'd been standing motionless for what seemed like an eternity in the hall just outside the room.

"Emma's awake, and she's going to be just fine," he assured them.

"Oh, thank God! Can we see her?" Lily asked, her eyes welled up with tears of joy."

"Yes, of course. Go right on in," Clem said. "Just try not to excite her too much."

Lily wiped at her eyes as she, Jack, and Keith hurried into the room. Jack stopped quickly on his way by to grab Clem's arm and mouth "thank you" to him, then followed his wife and son in to see his daughter.

Emma was propped up into a semi-reclined position. Her long brown hair was still matted and damp, her face was drained of all its normal coloring and her eyes were bloodshot, but at that moment she was the most beautiful sight her family had ever seen.

"Mom?" Emma called out, her voice hoarse.

Lily rushed over and hugged her, seriously contemplating never letting go of her again.

"Mom, I am so sorry..." Emma began, "I never should've..."

"Shhhh...it's all right, you don't have to say anything," her mom said. "We're just so thankful you're okay."

Emma then turned to her dad, who'd come around the other side of the bed. She grabbed onto his arm, holding on as tightly as she possibly could.

"Dad, I should've listened to you...I am so sorry," Emma said, tears streaming down her face.

He reached down and hugged her. Her mom grabbed a tissue from the bedside table and began wiping away her tears.

"Emma, all that matters is that you're all right. We love you so much," he said, smiling down at her.

"I love you both so much," Emma said, smiling for the first time since they'd walked into the room.

"Hey, what about me? Don't you love me too?" said Keith, grinning from ear to ear at his sister as he came closer to her bedside.

Emma managed a small chuckle. "Yes, even you," she said as she reached out her hand to him. Keith held on to it as tight as he could.

"And Ozzy too," she added.

A look of horror seized Keith's face. "Darn it! I forgot all about Ozzy! I've gotta go back for him; I left him tied at the beach!"

"No, you didn't; he's out in Clegg's truck," said Emma. As soon as the words came out, her experience came flooding back at her like a tidal wave.

"What are you talking about?" Keith said.

Emma hesitated. It was all too much to talk about. She had no words to describe what she'd just gone through. She wanted to fill them in on every last detail, yet another part of her imagined just how crazy it'd all sound. Am I crazy? Emma wondered. Did all of that really happen? But she knew beyond any shadow of a doubt that it did, but how would she ever convince anyone else of that? Certain everyone already thought she was flaky—which she kinda was—for diving off into water she knew held very real potential danger, she decided it'd be best to just keep it all to herself for now.

Before she could come up with anything in response to Keith's question, Clegg's voice could be heard from the doorway.

"She's right. Abby and I loaded him up into my truck before we left the lake and brought him here with us. The storm left the air nice and cool, so he's perfectly safe and sound out there. I'll bring him back to your house in a few minutes here, now that I know Emma's going to be okay."

"Thanks so much, Clegg," Keith said. "But I'm not so sure your truck will be okay after Ozzy gets done with it."

Clegg smiled. "No worries. I'm just so thankful that Emma's all right—that's all that matters," Clegg said, leaning against the doorway.

"Thank you," Emma said weakly, smiling back at him and also silently thanking him for interrupting at just the right time.

Keith looked as though he was in deep thought—which wasn't a common thing for him. He narrowed his eyes and looked at his sister. "Emma, how'd you know that Ozzy was out in Clegg's truck?"

Emma bit her lower lip. "Ummm…I just assumed he was? Clegg, did you say Abby came with you?" Emma said, trying to change the subject.

Keith continued to study Emma as if what she was saying didn't quite mesh with him but decided not to press her further.

Clegg nodded. "Yep, she's right out here."

"Can I please see her? Please?" Emma's eyes pleaded, looking back and forth between Clem and her mom.

Clem gave her a smile and nodded. "I don't see why not."

Abby, who'd been listening intently to the conversation from just outside the room, peeked her head in around the corner.

"Emma?" she squeaked. "Emma, I have never been happier to see you in my whole life!"

Emma smiled, holding out her arms to her. Lily moved out of the way as Abby dashed across the room, throwing her arms around Emma. They both burst into tears.

"I was so afraid I'd lost you!" Abby said.

"Don't get her too excited, okay, Abby?" Clem said. "Emma really needs her rest."

"I won't, Dad, I promise."

"Speaking of promises," Emma began, "can I please ask you all to promise me something?"

Before she could continue with her request, Emma sat forward and started coughing quite violently.

Emma's mom rushed back over to her side, patting her back and looking anxiously toward Clem.

"It's perfectly normal," Clem reassured her. "She may have some coughing spells like this for the next couple of days. Her lungs are irritated, and it'll take a while for them to fully recover. I'll get the nurse to give her something to help with that."

"Thank you, Clem," said Lily. He nodded in response and was just about to leave the room when Emma started to speak again.

"I need to ask you guys something, it's important," Emma said, struggling to get the words out between coughs.

"Shhhhh…just relax, honey, and try not to talk. Whatever it is can wait," her mom said.

"No, it can't! *Please* listen to me," Emma insisted, trying to hold back more coughing but not fully succeeding.

"All right, but let me get you some water first."

Her mom poured her a small glass from the pitcher on the bedside table. Emma sipped at the ice water, her cough eased for the moment. She sat back and began to speak, a look of urgency on her face.

"I need all of you to promise me you won't tell anyone else about any of this," she said as she started coughing again.

Her mother held out more water for her and Emma took another sip. "It's really important to me…I don't want people to know how stupid I was. *Please*." She looked around the room at everyone, her gaze coming to rest on Abby.

"Of course, we won't say anything if that's what you want," said Abby. "Right?"

Emma's parents, Keith, Clem, and Clegg all nodded in agreement.

"Thank you," Emma got out before the coughing came back again.

"I'll have the nurse bring that cough medicine in, then I want you to try to get some sleep, young lady. That's an order," Clem said, smiling down at Emma.

He noticed the look of concern on Lily's face. "Don't worry, Mom, she'll be good as new in just a couple days. I promise," he said, reaching out and squeezing her hand.

"Thank you, Clem…so much. For everything," Lily said, looking as if she was about to cry again.

Clem walked out through the door but not before he reminded Abby once more not to get Emma excited. Abby nodded.

"I didn't have a pulse, and he saved my life, didn't he?" Emma said after Clem was out in the hall.

"Yes, he did," her mom answered, a bit shocked, as no one had told her about that yet. "How did you know that?"

"I must've heard one of the nurses mention it," Emma said, looking down at her hands, which were shaking. She tried to steady them.

"I need to thank him…I owe him so much," Emma told her mom. Keith eyed her suspiciously.

"Clegg also saved your life," Keith added in. "You weren't breathing when they pulled you out of the lake. He gave you mouth to mouth."

Upon hearing this, tears began to form in Emma's eyes once more, and she began coughing again.

"Oh geez! I'm just about as dumb as they come. I never shoulda brought that up. At least not now," Keith said, looking worriedly at his sister.

"No, it's fine, Keith…I'm glad you told me."

"I love you, Emma," Keith suddenly blurted out. "Just needed to tell you that." For a brief moment a look of deep fondness passed between them.

"Gross," Emma said, giving him a small, sly smile. He laughed and winked in response.

"Clegg?" she said. "Thank you so much."

"You're more than welcome," Clegg said, "and now it's time for me to get that goat home while I still have a truck left to drive him home in."

This made Emma giggle, which of course made her cough even more. As if on cue, the nurse came into the room with the cough medicine.

"This is going to help your cough as well as help you to get some much needed sleep," the nurse said as she poured the dark green oozy stuff into a small cup.

"Glad you're the one downing that concoction and not me!" Keith said, pulling a face which made his sister smile. She took the medicine—which tasted even worse than it looked like it would—and was soon fast asleep.

Chapter 10

Emma gasped, bolting upright in bed; her heart beating a million miles a minute. It took her a couple of seconds to catch her breath. Only a nightmare she realized, breathing a deep sigh of relief. Looking around the room in her disoriented state, Emma noticed she wasn't in her bedroom but in a hospital room with her mom sprawled fast asleep in the chair next to the bed.

It swiftly occurred to her that all of this wasn't just a dream; it was also a real-life nightmare she'd just lived through several hours prior. *Thank God I lived through it*, she thought to herself. Then, suddenly, the recollection of the experience she had when her heart had stopped beating came back to her all over again.

"We've lost her!" she specifically recalled hearing someone say. Did she really die or was it just a dream? It couldn't have been a dream. All she knew was that it felt as real to her as anything she'd experienced—actually it felt *far* more real than anything she'd *ever* experienced in her entire life.

Then she began to think about what'd led up to it all and realized how very lucky she was to be alive. One horrendously stupid decision had nearly cost her life. Again she thanked God—literally—for allowing her a second chance. But she recalled the absolute helplessness and horror that washed over her as she struggled to untangle herself from the weeds as her lungs filled with water. It was all too much for Emma, and she suddenly began to cry hysterically—and cough.

Emma's mom instantly awoke upon hearing Emma's intense crying. She immediately got up and put her arms around her daughter.

"Oh, honey, I know...I know. Shhhh...it's all right now. You're okay, you're all right," Lily said. Emma clung to her mom tightly as if she were a life-preserver in a violent storm at sea.

"Mom, it was so awful!" Emma said, continuing to cry.

Becoming upset had caused her coughing to become so bad she was convulsing. Her mom called for the night nurse, who rushed in seconds later with more of the green goo. Emma took it, and within a moment her coughing subsided.

Lily held her and rocked her until Emma was fast asleep once more. She tucked her daughter in, then sat back down and watched her for the longest time. She felt deep sadness as she knew this experience would most likely change Emma forever. She was incredibly grateful not to be mourning the loss of her daughter, yet she was mourning the loss of that completely carefree little girl Emma might never be again.

Later on, after a couple of hours of tossing and turning, Emma woke up, unable to sleep anymore. She looked over at her mom and decided it'd be best to let her get some rest. Emma was about to get up and look for her mom's phone but thought better of it. It was just after midnight and even though she desperately wanted to talk to Abby, she knew Abby had to be asleep by now.

Abby eyed the numbers on her alarm clock; it was just after midnight, and she hadn't slept a wink. She couldn't stop thinking about everything Emma had just gone through.

Resigned that sleep wasn't going to happen, she threw back the covers, swung her feet around to the side of the bed, and stared out her window. She thought about how sometimes she and Emma would signal each other at night with flashlights as their rooms faced each other across the side yard. She'd give anything to be able to do that at this moment. The storm had finally cleared and the night sky was filled with stars—just as it had been the night of the fundraiser as she and Emma threw their message in a bottle into the lake.

Remembering that reminded Abby of the journal Emma had given to her as an early birthday present. The cover looked so much like the lake and the sky did that night. That night seemed like a thousand years ago. She wished she could magically turn back the clock.

She felt bad that she hadn't even written in the journal yet, but she imagined Emma had written in hers. Emma loved to write, and she was always making up funny little stories. Emma could always make Abby laugh, but yesterday for the first time she'd make her cry, which she felt on the verge of again. *Nearly losing a best friend can do that to you*, she told herself.

Her eyes were drawn down toward the drawer of her nightstand where she'd stashed away her journal the day Gretchen and her mom came over to check out the pool.

"What's that thing?" Gretchen had said as Abby walked into the house carrying the journal.

"It's an early birthday present from Emma," Abby said proudly. 'A journal."

"I have one of those, but I use it as a fashion planner," Gretchen said, practically whipping the thing out of Abby's hands to take a look.

"This one's plain and boring, though. Mine's bedecked with hundreds upon hundreds of bright pink sequins and sparkles," she said, haphazardly flinging Abby's journal onto a side table a few feet away.

"I love my journal. The cover's got special meaning for me and Emma. Excuse me for a moment," Abby said.

She picked up the journal and ascended the stairs as Gretchen looked indignant at being left standing there by herself. Abby brought it up to her room and put it in the drawer. Seething about Gretchen's rudeness, she sat down on the edge of her bed for a moment, trying to calm down. At that moment she figured she saw Gretchen in exactly the same way that Emma did and wondered if trying to be nice to her was even worth it.

Snapping out of her memory of that day, Abby turned on the light, took her journal out of the nightstand and grabbed a pen, then headed over to her window seat to curl up and write. She gazed out again at the moon and the stars for a few moments thinking about how to put what she wanted to say.

At last, Abby opened her journal to the first page and put pen to paper.

Something unthinkable happened today…Emma nearly drowned. She dove off the diving board at the lake, got stuck in the weeds, and when they pulled her up she wasn't breathing. I was there, and it ripped my heart out to see her like that. Uncle Clegg saved her and got her breathing again. Then at the hospital, her heart stopped beating. I've never been more afraid in my life. Thank God Dad was able to save her.

This is all my fault because I could've saved her from having any of this happen to begin with if I'd just gone back out in the water like she'd asked me to. Some best friend I am.

I'm still so shaken up over this. I can't believe she took a risk like that just to practice her dives. And for what? She's the best diver on the team.

I gave Emma my word I'd never breathe a word of this to anyone, I just hope she'll never take a chance like this ever, again. So very, very thankful that she's okay.

Abby closed her journal and hugged it tightly as if the words inside brought her closer to Emma while she stared out at the night sky once more.

Back at the hospital, Emma stared out her window. The storm had been over with for several hours, and she saw the clear night sky revealing a multitude of stars. She wished the memory of what'd happened to her at the lake could've dissipated as easily as the storm clouds.

Her dad had gone home earlier to get some of her things, and Emma remembered asking if he could bring her new journal back to her. She surveyed the room for it, in the eerie, clinical glow of the dimmed fluorescent hospital lights. She spotted it on the side table next to some lovely flower arrangements she hadn't previously noticed.

One was an extravagant, multi-colored bouquet of roses from the O'Donnells in a heart-shaped vase; another was a smaller, yet just as beautiful bouquet of daffodils in a smiley-face vase from her parents; and the third—which made her laugh—were a bunch of mom's daisies in a drinking glass from home, from Keith, with a note that read, "Picked them before Ozzy could eat them!"

She reached for her journal, almost knocking over the bigger bouquet onto her mom's head but steadied it just in time, then opened the side table drawer to hunt for something to write with. She pulled out a small eraser-less pencil—the kind that almost doesn't qualify to be a pencil; the kind people use to keep bowling scores with—and opened her journal. She stared back out the window, shivering momentarily. Not because the room was cold but because thinking too hard about what had happened chilled her to the bone.

My mind is spinning from everything that's happened today…

I almost drowned, but Clegg and Abby's dad both saved my life. Clegg got me breathing again at the lake when they got me out of the water and Clem brought me back to life when my heart stopped. MY HEART STOPPED. I am so thankful to be alive right now. How can I ever repay them?

None of this would've happened if I hadn't been so stupid… I'm still shaking just thinking about it. I will never take another chance like that. Ever.

And then there's what happened to me when my heart had stopped. Was I really in the presence of God? I felt sure I was—and still do—but have I lost my mind?

Before that I floated above everything and saw and heard things I couldn't have known about. I remember the pain people felt and then Ozzy seeing me. He actually saw me!

Then the whole thing with the tunnel and then light. It was so much more than a light. And the way everything felt. I remember having a choice to stay or not…I'm way too tired to try to put any of this into words. All I can say is I am just blown away and very, very thankful to God that I'm still here.

Emma sat for a moment trying to decide if there was anything else she wanted to write. There wasn't, so she closed the journal and put it back on the bedside table. She thought her first journal entry would be about some great, fun adventure she and Abby had together. Never in a billion years did she imagine it would be anything like this.

Falling back asleep shortly afterward, Emma slept soundly till almost noon.

She awoke feeling much stronger and very eager to get out the hospital—and all that it stood for—and get back home. However, Clem came in and laid down the law, telling her she had to stay one more night so they could keep an eye on her. Her mom wholeheartedly agreed, but Emma had other ideas.

"Aw, come on! I really wanna go home today, please? I'm feeling lots better. You live right next door if I started feeling worse…" Emma pleaded with him, but he interrupted her, remaining adamant.

"You may be feeling better—and that's the best news I could hear—but you're still weak and after everything you went through…well, I just want to keep you here for one more night so I can release you tomorrow morning with a clean bill of health," he said.

From behind his back he produced her favorite double-chocolate ice cream sundae from the ice cream shop around the corner from the hospital.

Emma's eyes lit up. "Thanks!" she said, her voice still a bit scratchy.

"Abby insisted I bring you one. It'll also help your throat feel better. Just don't let it get out that I brought my favorite patient her favorite ice cream. The other patients might get jealous," he said, winking.

"My lips are sealed," she said, giggling. "Or, they will be once I finish this."

He turned to leave, but she continued, "I don't know how to thank you, Clem. And I don't just mean about the ice cream…"

He turned back around, smiling warmly. "I know, and you're welcome."

Chapter 11

The following week, Clegg was back in town and swim practice resumed at the lake. The surrounding area was beginning to take shape: most of the new boards were in place on the dock, much of the debris had been cleared from the beach, the snack shack looked a lot less like a shack now and they were just starting to tackle the landscaping.

Emma was "as fit as a fiddle" now, according to Clem, and cleared to do whatever she wanted—including swimming. Although Emma wasn't so sure "swimming" still fell under the category of "things she wanted to do." In fact, she'd been awake most of the night worrying about it.

"I think it'll be good for you to get right back into the water," her mom said, noticing the expression on Emma's face when they arrived at the lake that morning.

"I'll be right here doing some planting, your dad will be working on the dock, Abby's here, and Clegg will be keeping a very close eye on you. Please don't let what happened keep you from doing what you love."

Emma gave her mom a half-hearted smile and hugged her before getting out of their SUV. "Love you, Mom."

"Love you, too. Have a great time!" Her mom said, smiling reassuringly.

Emma turned and started down the beach toward where the rest of the swim team had gathered. Her mom's smile was quickly replaced by a look of apprehension. Emma had no clue that her mom had no plans of doing anything else at the lake that day other than watching her daughter like a hawk.

Dropping her backpack and towel down on the beach, Emma sat down in the sand a bit farther back from the rest of the girls, who were gathered in front of Clegg as he addressed them.

"Okay, girls, listen up…this is very important. We've put up a sign up on the floating dock as a reminder that the water on the other side is *off limits*. The area is also clearly marked and roped off from the rest of the lake. The weeds are very thick and tangled over there, and it is not safe for anyone to be over there." He briefly looked in Emma's direction, who immediately cast her eyes downward.

"If you see anyone in that vicinity tell them to get out, then alert me immediately. We've got people coming out to get rid of the weeds, but until then that area is off limits. Understood?"

Once again, the row of bobble-head dolls compliantly showed they understood.

"All righty then," Clegg continued, "let's hit the water and have some fun!"

The girls scrambled up out of the sand, eager to get back into the lake again—all of them except Emma. She slowly and deliberately tried to stall, pretending—in a highly exaggerated fashion—to look for some imaginary lost object in her backpack. As the other girls jumped into the water, amid much chatter and splashing, Abby came over to see Emma.

"Hey, watcha looking for?" Abby asked.

"Huh? Oh, ummm, nothing." Even so, she continued to dig furiously.

Realizing how lame that must've seemed, she flung her backpack down into the sand while Abby eyed her. Emma knew she was on to her.

"You're a little nervous about getting back in, aren't you…?" Abby asked. Emma looked away.

"It'll be okay, I promise," Abby said, smiling warmly, reaching out to briefly squeeze Emma's hand.

Emma turned back toward Abby and gave her a huge smile that came nowhere near to reaching her eyes. "You're right. It's gonna be fun."

She could see Abby wasn't falling for it and was clearly still scrutinizing her. *Sometimes it can really stink to have someone who knows you better than you know yourself*, Emma thought.

"Really, it's all good. Let's just get in the water," Emma said, trying to wipe the doubt off Abby's face.

"All right, but I'll be right there with you, okay?"

"Honestly, Abby, I'm not a baby. I've can do this."

"I know you can, but it's all right to admit that you're scared, you know. I would be too," Abby said.

Emma wasn't going to admit to anything of the sort.

"Last one in's got goat's breath!" Emma said suddenly, then took off toward the water.

"Hey, now that's the Emma I know and love!" Abby said, surprised at the turnaround.

Making it to the water first, Abby jumped right in. Emma came to a screeching halt at the water's edge and froze. To say she was gripped in fear would be a serious understatement.

A feeling so intense consumed her that she honestly wondered if she were about to die. Her heart beat loudly, rapidly, and erratically. She was clenched by an all-encompassing nausea. Pins and needles attacked her limbs. A sensation of unreality set in as dizziness so severe made her feel as though her surroundings were spinning out of control. Emma felt faint and in that instance plunked herself down on the ground, fearing she was going to pass out.

Emma's mom dashed down the beach toward her daughter. At the same time Abby noticed Emma was still up on the beach, sitting in the sand looking very distressed.

"Emma?" Lily called out. She didn't respond and appeared to be in a daze. Abby made haste up to the shore.

"Emma, you okay?" her mom said, kneeling in front of her. Just then, Abby appeared and knelt down in front of Emma as well. Emma blinked her eyes a few times, snapping out of it.

"What just happened to me?" Emma asked in great alarm.

"I'm sure it's nothing to worry about. Maybe it really was just too soon for you to be out here," her mom said, trying not to show the overwhelming worry she felt as she didn't want to upset Emma further. She sat next to her, putting an arm around her daughter's shoulders.

Emma looked around and noticed some of the other girls noticing her sitting there. She sat up a little straighter, hoping they wouldn't catch on that something was wrong.

"I'm really not feeling very well, Mom. At all. I thought I was gonna faint," Emma said, the color completely drained from her face.

Leaning into her mom, she began feeling lightheaded all over again. Lily turned to call out to her husband, but he was already at their side.

"I'm sure she's okay, but I think we need to call Clem," Lily said, trying to sound calm for Emma's sake.

Jack could tell she felt anything but calm. He quickly got out his phone.

"Come on, let's get you to the car." Lily helped Emma to stand up.

"I'm coming with you guys," said Abby.

"No, Abby. It's okay, I'll be fine. Please, just stay here and have a good practice," Emma said.

"No way. I'm coming with you to make sure you're all right," Abby insisted.

"If you come, they're gonna think it's a big deal," she said, pointing out at the girls in the water, "and I don't want that. You need to stay here so if they ask, you can just tell them I'm coming down with a cold or something. Please?"

Abby didn't want to, but she conceded to her friend's wishes. "Fine. I'll stay, but I don't want to. I'll come over straight after practice," she said.

Abby reached out and hugged Emma, noticing how cold and clammy she felt. It scared her to death. Emma's dad gathered up her things as her mom helped her up the beach.

Gretchen, treading water a slight distance away, had been studying the whole situation with great interest. Abby stood watching as Emma and her parents made their way up the beach. Gretchen swam toward the shore, climbed out of the water and came up next to Abby.

"So what's wrong with her?" Abby nearly jumped out of her skin as she had no idea Gretchen was there.

"Oh, she's…just coming down with something is all," Abby answered.

"Probably some kind of weird goat germ disease," Gretchen said, laughing. "Come on, let's get back in the water!"

She seriously considered telling Gretchen off but let it pass as she knew it wouldn't help anyone. Her concern for Emma encompassed her. Abby stood for another moment watching as the Rhodes' drove off. She turned to find Gretchen was still standing there as well, so she gave her a half-hearted smile and headed back down to the water with her.

When Jack called Clem he was instructed to bring Emma into the office immediately. As they got to the SUV, she started to feel a bit better, but she was completely exhausted. She fell asleep instantly and stayed out like a light until they reached the office ten minutes later.

"Emma? We're here," Lily said, gently shaking her daughter's shoulder to wake her.

"Huh?" she said slowly opening her eyes and looking around. "Where are we?"

"We're at Clem's office," her dad told her.

"Oh," she said, sitting up straighter in her seat, "I remember now. I think I'm feeling lots better, actually," she said, hoping beyond all hope to get out of going in.

"I'm so glad, but we really need to get you checked out just to make sure you're okay, especially after all you've been through."

Emma sighed, reluctantly getting out of the SUV. Once they were inside—unlike any time anyone ever goes to the doctor—Emma was seen immediately. After a thorough examination, Clem declared her absolutely fine—at least physically.

"Then why did I feel like I was gonna die?" Emma asked.

"As you said, you felt perfectly fine until you were about to get into the water, am I right?"

Emma nodded.

"Then you felt terrified when you were about to get in, and that's when the physical symptoms occurred."

"Yes."

"Emma, what you experienced was panic attack.

"So you mean I'm crazy?" Emma said, looking horrified.

"No, Emma, not at all…" he said smiling, trying to reassure her as he sat down next to her. "It was in response to the idea of getting in the water. You're frightened that what happened to you that day at the lake will happen to you again. So you've developed an overwhelming fear of getting back into the water—a perfectly natural reaction under the circumstances—which manifest itself into physical symptoms. That's basically what a panic attack is."

Emma broke down. "I am very, *very* afraid that it will happen again, and I never want to get back in the water, not ever!" Her mom put an arm around her shoulder.

"It's not uncommon to feel this way, especially after going through something so traumatic. Given time, these feelings may very well pass," Clem told her.

"I can't imagine ever feeling any differently about it," Emma said, her shoulders slumped. "Can we please go now?"

"Yes, of course. But Emma? You've always loved the water, and you're a strong swimmer. You just need to give it some time, for now," he said, standing up and getting the door for her.

She nodded her head doubtfully, looking down at the floor.

"Would you mind waiting out in the waiting room with your dad? I just want to talk to your mom for a moment."

"Sure."

"I'll be right out, honey," her mom said.

Emma left the room, and Clem closed the door behind her. He sat back down, folding his arms in front of him.

"I didn't want to say this in front of Emma as I don't want her to give up hope, but due to the extreme circumstances she went through there's a possibility she may never get over this fear. Sometimes therapy can help but not always. Especially in a case like hers. I just wanted you and Jack to be know so you can be prepared."

"Thanks, Clem, I appreciate you telling me," Lily said, taking a deep breath. "It tears me apart trying to imagine what all this must be like for her."

"I know."

Little did either one of them know that Emma had overheard every word they'd just said.

Not long after Emma and her parents got home, there was a knock at the door—it was Abby. Keith answered the door wearing his headphones.

"*HEY, ABBY!*" he yelled in order to hear himself over the music while he gestured her inside. She could quite easily hear the nonsensical shrieking of heavy metal from five feet away.

"EMMA'S UP IN HER ROOM IF YOU WANNA GO SEE HER!" Keith informed her, still yelling at the top of his lungs above the deafening racket being pumping into his ears.

"Ummm…you don't have to yell," Abby said, amused.

"WHAT? I CAN'T HEAR YOU!" Keith yelled once more. At last it dawned on him to take off the earphones. "Oops…sorry 'bout that," Keith said, smiling cheekily.

Abby smiled in return shaking her head. "How's she doing?"

"She's really tired, but Mom said your dad checked her out and she's A- OK. But I guess she's really freaked out about getting back in the water."

Abby went up the stairs and saw Emma's door ajar. Emma looked like she fast asleep with Ozzy curled up next to her, snoring away like a chainsaw. Abby couldn't help but chuckle, which woke him up. He opened up one eye, regarded Abby, then closed it again and began snoring again almost instantly. Abby quietly closed the door behind her and headed back down the stairs.

After Abby shut the door, Emma opened her eyes. She'd been in and out of sleep but awake when Abby walked in. She was thinking about what she'd overheard Clem say to her mom and didn't really felt like talking to anyone. She sighed deeply and looked over at Ozzy.

As if he sensed her looking at him, he suddenly woke up raised his head and looked at her.

"You really saw me that day, didn't you, Ozzy…?" Emma asked him incredulously.

Ozzy nodded slightly, then slid over closer to her, put his head on her shoulder and fell back asleep. Within minutes, Emma did too.

"THAT WAS QUICK!" Keith yelled once more out of the blue, startling her right out of her skin and back again. He popped his headphones back off.

"Oops, sorry 'bout that again," he said in a normal volume, offering her a big goofy grin.

"She was asleep—although I can't imagine how with you yelling your face off like that," Abby teased.

"You wanna listen to some awesome metal with me?" Keith asked as if it were actually a possibility.

"Ahhh…thanks, but I'd rather listen to someone scratch their fingernails down a chalkboard," she said, smiling, and taking this as a good opportunity to leave.

"You just don't appreciate good quality music," he said.

Abby rolled her eyes, smiled again, and waved as she let herself out the front door. He waved back to her, put his headphones back on and wildly bobbed his head up and down to the beat.

Chapter 12

Emma and Abby sat together in the shade of the patio table's umbrella, overlooking the pool in the O'Donnell's backyard as they pored through a scrapbook their moms put together for them of when the girls were much younger. The sun blazed hot with a nasty vengeance, giving way to the kind of day which would allow a person to make pancakes on the hood of a car if they so desired.

The pool was resort-worthy in both size and beauty. A major part of their summers together since they were very young were spent here, with Emma spending just as much time in it —if not more—than Abby.

"Oh my goodness! Look at this one," Abby said, pointing to a picture of much younger versions of the two of them in identical mermaid costumes. "We were about three, remember? It was our first time ever trick-or-treating."

"How could I forget? We had no idea we'd be wearing the same exact getup. Mom said everyone kept getting us mixed up," Emma said, smiling.

Abby flipped through a couple more pages then stopped at a photo in which their expressions were a stark contrast to one another.

"Here's that time when we got our ears pierced," Abby said.

"I remember that *all* too well. I cried my face off 'cause it hurt like crazy, and you didn't even feel a thing. I still have those earrings by the way."

"Oh wow, so do I!"

Abby's mom stuck her head out the French doors to the patio. "Lunch will be ready in a couple of minutes. You girls want to eat out here?"

"Yes, please," said Abby.

She went back to thumbing through the scrapbook. "Okay, this one's got to be one of my very favorites. Look at that, our first attempts at diving—well, if you can call them dives. We both cannonballed into the deep end together, remember? Look at your face, it's all scrunched up like a prune! I love it!" Abby said, laughing heartily.

She glanced over at Emma who wasn't sharing Abby's sentiments at all. In fact, she looked like she might be sick.

"Emma, what's wrong…you okay?" Abby asked.

Emma looked away.

"I am so stupid. That picture reminded you of what happened, didn't it…I am so sorry, I never should've gotten the scrapbook out."

Emma turned back to face Abby. "No, it's fine. You're not stupid for getting the scrapbook out. I'm stupid for doing what I did."

"Abby, I gotta tell you something, and you've gotta promise me you won't tell anyone, cause if anyone knew they'd think I was completely pathetic," Emma paused, looking at Abby.

"Of course, I won't tell anyone…what is it?"

"There's absolutely no way I'm getting back in the water. Ever. I completely freak out just thinking about it," she said, looking as if she was about to cry.

"Oh, Emma, I am so very sorry," Abby said, looking at her friend with deep concern.

"The first day back at practice after it happened, you know, when we ran to the water? I froze in terror when I got to the edge. My heart pounded so hard and so fast I thought it was gonna stop again. I felt like I was gonna be sick, faint, and die all at the same time…it was awful! Your dad told me it was a panic attack." Emma started to cry.

Abby moved over to give her a hug. "Emma, there's got to be some way to get you over this. I don't know of anyone who loves the water more than you do."

"Not anymore I don't."

"What can I do to help?"

"I don't think there's anything anyone can do to help. There's just totally no way I'm ever getting back in the water. I've had nightmares every night about it happening all over again."

"That must be horrible for you…maybe my dad can find someone for you to talk to about it. He knows some people who…"

"No!" Emma said adamantly. "I don't want to talk to anyone about it. Just talking about it makes me feel like I'll have another panic attack."

"Oh, Emma, I am so very sorry…I really wish I knew what to do or say. I really can't help but feel that this is all my fault."

"Huh?" Emma said, not understanding what Abby was getting at.

"Okay, ladies, lunch is served!" Abby's mom said, unintentionally interrupting as she carried out a tray of sandwiches, salads, milk and cookies for the girls, but stopped in her tracks when she noticed the look on Emma's face.

"Emma, what's wrong?"

"Nothing really…I'm just being silly," Emma said, not wanting to discuss it with her.

A look of concern passed between Abby and her mom.

"You sure?" Abby's mom asked.

"Yep, I'm good," Emma said, forcing a smile. "Hey, those sandwiches look delicious," she said, trying to change the subject. "Peanut butter and jelly's been my favorite since forever."

"I know. I also remember when you were younger that you not only liked to eat peanut butter, but you also enjoyed finger painting with it on your mom's kitchen walls, much to her dismay." Abby's mom said, teasing Emma.

This brought a genuine smile to Emma's face. "I totally saw nothing wrong with it at the time. We're still trying to break Keith of that habit, though."

All three of them giggled while Elaine set the table and spread out the food.

"It's a real scorcher today, you girls should get in the pool after lunch and get cooled off."

A quick look of dread washed over Emma's face, which wasn't lost on Abby or her mom.

"Ummm...that's okay, Mom, I think we'd just prefer to sit here in the shade for today."

"Suit yourselves, but I think it's the first time I've ever known the two of you to pass up going in the pool—especially on a day like this," Abby's mom said, trying to not let on that she could now pretty much see—to some extent—what might be going on with Emma.

"Maybe the two of you could just sit at the shallow end and dangle your feet in to get cooled off?"

"Yeah, maybe..." Abby said.

She and her mom exchanged knowing looks while Emma looked over toward the pool, flinching visibly.

"Okay, well...if you need anything else I'll be in the kitchen baking some pies to take over to the nursing home later, when I go to pick up Cameron.

"Thanks, Mom."

"Yes, thank you," said Emma.

"You're welcome, and Emma? If you ever want to talk about anything—anything at all—you know I'm always here for you, right?"

"I know you are," Emma said quietly, looking away from Abby's mom. "Thanks."

Abby and her mom exchanged looks again, then she went back into the house to leave the two girls to their lunch.

Emma picked up her sandwich, was about to take a bite, then put it back down again.

"You okay?" asked Abby.

Emma looked uneasy. "Something else I need to tell you about..."

Abby put her sandwich down as well and regarded her friend intently. "What is it?"

"You'll think I've totally gone off the deep end..."

"No, I won't, Emma. Just tell me, please?"

Emma paused for a moment. "I'll tell you, but you've got to also promise me that you won't breathe a word of this to anyone."

"I promise," Abby assured her.

"Something really, truly weird happened when my heart had stopped," Emma said, looking down at her hands, which were shaking again. "Something beyond weird."

"What was it?" Abby said with a note of concern as she also noticed Emma's hands shaking.

Emma proceeded to tell Abby every last detail she could remember of her experience. Abby sat mesmerized, listening to the whole thing without saying a word. When she was finished, Abby had tears in her eyes. She got up and gave Emma a hug. Emma began to cry as well.

After both girls got a grip, Abby went back over to her chair and sat down. "Wow. I don't even know what to say," Abby said, still in shock.

"Yeah, I know. It's out there. You don't think I've lost it, do you?"

"No, Emma, not at all. My dad's told us of several patients he's heard about who've experienced almost exactly what you did."

"Are you kidding me? So I'm really not crazy after all?" Emma said, looking like the weight of the world had been lifted off her shoulders.

"Well, you *are* crazy but that's not why," Abby teased, lightening the atmosphere.

"Thank you so much for listening to all this and for not thinking I'd lost my mind."

"I'm trying to imagine what it was all like for you. Have you told your family?"

"I'm afraid they'd think I had a few screws loose, or worse yet that I was making it up," Emma said, genuinely concerned.

"You need to stop doubting yourself, nobody would think that of you," Abby said, trying to encourage Emma.

"Maybe you should doubt me *more* than you do after the stupid stunt I pulled the other day."

"Hey, we all make mistakes," Abby said.

"Yeah, but not usually ones *that* stupid. If they did the human race might be extinct by now."

"What you did may have been stupid, but you certainly aren't. Anyway, I totally think you should talk to my dad about what happened—tell him everything you told me," Abby said.

"I dunno…it's seriously hard to talk about, and what if he thinks I'm nuts or making it up?"

"Emma, he won't. I promise you. Plus, there's a guy he knows who's doing research on this kind of thing. They call what happened to you a near-death experience."

"A near-death experience?"

"Yup, and lots of people have had them," she said, trying to reassure her friend. "Please think about talking to him. I think it would really help you to hear what he has to say."

Emma thought about it for a moment. "Maybe I should talk to him; it'd be kinda cool to find out more about what happened with these other people."

"I know he'll be free after work tomorrow night, why don't you hang around and talk to him after the party?"

"Maybe I will," Emma said, smiling. "Oh wow, I almost forgot—tomorrow's your birthday!"

"That's 'cause you're an awful friend," Abby said, teasing again. "Seriously, you've had more than enough going on lately. I can hardly blame you for not remembering."

Emma got up from the table. "I've gotta get home; I'm feeling a bit tired."

"You okay?"

"Yeah, just talking about all this kinda wore me out," said Emma. "Thanks again for listening to me go on and on and on about it, *and* for not thinking I'm nuts. You're the best friend anyone could ever ask for. I mean that."

"So are you," said Abby. "I'll see you tomorrow, then?"

"Yep, bright and early, birthday girl!"

Emma turned to make her way out of the O'Donnell's backyard and into her own. Abby watched after her, feeling so incredibly thankful her best friend was still alive.

Chapter 13

Much later that evening, Abby could not get to sleep so she curled up on the window seat with her journal. She couldn't stop thinking about all that Emma had confided to her today, about her panic attacks *and* her near-death experience.

She stared out at the calm surface of the pool water, thinking of the sharp contrast between that and the disturbance she'd seen in the lake where Emma had dived in. She shuddered and looked away quickly. She thought that if she could feel like this about it, she couldn't even begin to imagine how Emma must feel and how bad her fear of the water must be now.

My heart is breaking for Emma. No one could ever keep her out of the water—or get her out once she was in it—but now I'm afraid she'll never get back in.

Abby looked over toward the Rhode's house. She saw a soft glow of light emanating from Emma's bedroom window and wondered if Emma was also having trouble sleeping or if her light was on because she'd just awoke from another nightmare. She truly hoped the latter wasn't the case.

She's terrified of going in the water now, to the point of having really bad panic attacks. She says she's never going back in the water again. I wish I knew how to help. None of this would be going on if I'd just kept up my end of the pact. She told me not to tell anyone 'cause she thinks people will think she's pathetic. Can't imagine anyone being so cruel, but just the same I'll never tell.

And I get chills thinking about what happened to her while her heart had stopped beating—she had a near-death experience! I cannot get over how incredible it all is—it's like something out of a crazy dream. I'm the only one she's told 'cause she's afraid everyone will think she's crazy or that she's lying. All anyone would have to do is listen to her talk about it to know it really, truly happened. I promised to keep it a secret, and I will, but I really think she should talk to my dad about it.

Emma was completely exhausted but sitting upright in bed with her light on. She was determined to fight off sleep tonight as she wanted nothing to do with the nightmare that kept coming back every night since she nearly drowned.

She looked down to the foot of her bed where Ozzy lay curled up and snoring. Normally he slept in her brother's room, but he'd been her constant nighttime companion since she'd gotten home from the hospital. Even though Ozzy was Keith's partner in crime, he'd always felt protective of Emma, but they had even more of a connection since she saw him that day in Clegg's truck, and she knew he'd seen her. He also seemed to have a real sense that things weren't quite right with her lately.

Emma reached over onto her nightstand and picked up her journal, looking at the cover. It amazed and horrified her that the simple, tranquil beauty of a lake could encompass the dangers it does just below the surface. Emma adjusted her pillows behind her back, opened up the journal, and began to write.

I finally told Abby that I'm never getting back in the water. I also told her what her dad said about me having a panic attack. I hated telling her as I knew how bad she'd feel for me, but at the same time I had to tell her—she's my best friend. She wants to help but there's nothing she or anyone else can do. I'm terrified of the water, and I always will be. I made her promise to tell no one.

I also spilled my guts to her about what happened. She says they call it a near-death experience and lots of people have had them, and that I should talk to her dad about it. I'm so glad I was able to finally get it all out. I made her promise not to tell anyone about that too, although I now realize asking Abby to keep my secrets is like asking a dog to wag its tail. I'm so lucky I have her to confide in.

Emma paused for a moment, looking out the window. She saw Abby's light was on and wondered what she was doing up.

If any of this got out, everyone—especially Gretchen—would think I was completely pathetic.

Emma's eyelids started getting heavy, and she felt herself beginning to doze off. Suddenly, she jerked awake, startling Ozzy, who sprang up on all fours—in turn startling Emma. He then nudged Emma with his head, and she patted him. After assessing that all was good, he groaned, laid back down and began snoring again, almost instantly. Soon Emma was fighting to stay awake once more, only this time sleep won the battle.

The nightmare came back again shortly after she fell asleep. She gasped upon awakening as usual, as if she never took a single breath during the whole dream. Ozzy sprang up beside her, licking her face vigorously as he'd done every time she awoke from that same nightmare. She hugged him tight, and he settled in beside her, his head resting on hers. She lay wide awake like that for hours while Ozzy slipped back into sleep and snored once more. Once daybreak arrived, she got up, severely tired from a lack of sleep but in spite of that she was excited, for it was the day of Abby's birthday party.

Chapter 14

"**M**ake a wish and blow out the candles!" Abby's mom told her daughter. Keith's band just finished their rendition of "Happy Birthday"—heavy metal style—much to the dismay of Ozzy's ears.

Everybody cheered and clapped as Abby blew out the candles on her cake. "Everyone" consisted of the entire swim team, Abby and Emma's moms, Cameron, Keith, and his band. They all had on party hats—even Ozzy. He'd taken the liberty of eating the first two they'd given him but apparently lost his appetite for them by the time the third one made an appearance.

They were celebrating Abby's birthday party in the O'Donnell's backyard, around the pool. There was a giant, inflatable birthday cake making its way around the pool while a banner proclaiming *HAPPY BIRTHDAY, ABBY!* was splayed across the back fence. Balloons and streamers decorated the entire area in a simple, yet festive, way. A piñata in the shape of a goat hung haplessly off a flagpole— awaiting a doom it could do nothing about—which Ozzy had briefly regarded with a look of disdain. The girls from the swim team were dressed up in a wide variety of fancy party dresses with Gretchen's sticking out like a sore thumb in an eye assaulting bright blinding yellow.

"Whaddya wish for?" Gretchen asked.

"Can't tell you, it's a secret," Abby said looking over in Emma's direction, which Gretchen picked up on.

"Oh, of course you can!" Gretchen insisted.

"Nope, sorry," Abby said as Gretchen gave her an indignant scowl.

"Time for cake, everyone!" announced Abby's mom, cutting the cake as Emma's mom held out plates for her to put the slices on.

The band abandoned their instruments and left them for dead at the mention of cake. Keith called out to Ozzy—who'd been wandering around "mowing" the confines of the O'Donnell's fenced-in backyard—to come join them. Gretchen heard this and marched over to confront Keith.

"Why in the world did you bring that stupid, nasty, germ-ridden mule to the party?" she said, placing her hands on her hips to show him this was serious, and she meant business.

"Hey, keep it down, he can hear you," Keith said as Ozzy cocked his party hat adorned head to one side, listening intently to the exchange.

"First off, he was invited, second, he's not a mule—he's a goat. And third, he's got *far* better manners than you do!" Keith said, offering her a sardonic smile.

"I'll never understand why Abby wastes her time associating with the likes of you, your dumb goat, *or* your stupid sister," Gretchen said, scrunching up her face into an exaggerated look of revulsion. "And why do you always wear that stupid denim vest, anyway?"

"You know, if you keep makin' that face you're going to look like a wrinkled-up old lady before you're even fifteen," Keith remarked.

Gretchen's expression immediately turned to concern as her hands flew up to feel her face all over for signs of lines and creases. Keith chuckled when it finally dawned on Gretchen she was being duped. She shot him a nasty look then whipped her head around and stalked off toward the cake table.

Cameron, who'd been listening to the whole thing, came over to Keith. "She really is something else, isn't she...?" Cameron said as they both scrutinized her from a distance.

"She sure is." Keith stared off into the distance for a moment.

Cameron sniffed the air. "Where the heck did that nasty smell come from?"

"I'm thinkin' it came from Gretchen—it was way worse when she was standin' right in front of me. That girl must've bathed in some seriously bad perfume."

"It smells worse than a skunk!" Cameron said, trying not to breathe through his nose.

"Yeah, it's pretty rank. For some weird reason it smells familiar, though."

A gleam appeared in his eyes as the corners of his mouth slowly turning up into a dastardly devious grin. "I've come up with a fiendishly delightful way to get her, but I'll be needin' your help."

Cameron smiled wickedly. "Oh, this should be good; tell me..."

Keith leaned down and murmured something into Cameron's ear. Soon they were both cracking up.

"This is gonna be epic," said Cameron.

"Indeed," agreed Keith. "Now let's go snag some cake before those girls wolf it all down...I promised Ozzy a piece."

Keith weaved his way through the sea of girls and was easily able to cut in line as all but three of those girls— Emma, Abby and Gretchen—thought him to be the most amazing creature to walk the face of the planet. Keith came back to where Cameron and Ozzy awaited him, handing Cameron his piece and sitting another plate of cake down on the ground for the goat. Ozzy's piece was gone instantly but left him with a frosting mustache, which he noisily licked at for a good two minutes.

"I'm thinkin' Ozzy here's gettin' a bit too plump for his own good. After today, I'm gonna have to seriously cut back on his snacks," Keith told Cameron.

Ozzy looked up, both alarmed and thoroughly dejected.

"Well, time to get back to makin' some music...I think we should plan for Operation Gretchen during the next break."

"Sounds good to me," Cameron said.

They both mock saluted each other as Keith went back to where the band was set up over by the deep end of the pool.

Nothing of much consequence happened for the next half hour or so during the band's set as the partygoers continued to eat cake and ice cream, chatting amongst themselves and listening to the music while a few lovesick girls took videos—as well as about a hundred thousand pictures—of Keith and his band while they performed.

"We're gonna be takin' another break now, but don't all you girls get to worryin', there'll still be more awesome music to come!" Keith announced into the microphone.

Two girls ran up to Keith, pathetically gushing about his guitar playing while he soaked it all up like a giant sea sponge. Keith spotted Cameron looking over at him and gave him a knowing nod. Cameron gave it back to him.

"Sorry, girls, I've got some ultra-important business to take care of!"

At the same time, Ozzy had his front hooves up on a table overflowing with presents and was just about to select one for himself when Keith caught him in the act. "Oh, no you don't, Ozz-man. Besides, I've got some fun in store for you."

With a sudden twinkle in his eye, the goat quickly put his front legs back down on the ground and trotted toward Keith with eager anticipation.

"Follow me," Keith said. He gave a knowing nod to Cameron to let the games begin.

"Hey, you know what?" Cameron said loudly, addressing the all the girls, "You all look *so* lovely today in your beautiful party dresses that I've totally got to get a picture of everyone together!" Cameron beckoned to them, trying his very best to sound flattering.

All the girls were instantly flattered, except for Emma and Abby who knew something was definitely up. They raised their eyebrows and looked at each other.

"Ummmm…really? What is up with Cameron?" Emma asked. "When does he ever think girls getting all dressed up is anything short of stupid?"

They eyed him suspiciously, seeing straight through his fake angelic expression while the rest of the girls—not suspecting a thing—excitedly primped for their upcoming photo-op.

"He's totally up to something…I just don't know what it is yet. I do, however, get the feeling we'll find out soon enough," said Abby.

Cameron glanced in Abby's direction—feeling his sister's eyes boring into him like a dentist's drill into a bad cavity. He attempted an innocent smile.

"And no doubt Keith's in on it as well," said Emma as they both simultaneously shifted their gaze to him. He must've sensed it because he turned around and smiled sheepishly at them.

"Mom, can I borrow your phone so I can use the camera?" Cameron asked.

"Of course…but what are you up to?" his mom said, eyeing him.

"Why, Mom, just attempting to capture all this beauty on film is all," Cameron said, smiling brightly.

"Mhmmm…" she said, handing him her phone. "What are you and Keith in cahoots about this time?"

"Keith and I? *In cahoots?* Now what would make you even ask such a thing..." Cameron said, giving his mom a crafty look as he turned and hurried off.

Meanwhile, the girls continued to fuss with themselves—in the way all girls who know they're about to be photographed have the inborn need to do—as Cameron went over near the pool.

"Okay, everyone, come stand over here in front of the pool," Cameron called out.

He began to fiddle with the phone, looking a little confused as the giggling girls positioned and posed themselves poolside. Emma placed herself as far away from the pool as she possibly could without making her intentions too obvious to anyone.

"Hmmm...I'm just not sure how this thing works. Keith, can you lend me a hand?"

"Of course," but only if Ozzy can get his handsome mug in the picture as well. He'd be one very offended goat if he couldn't."

"Well, by all means then. Join in, Ozzy," Cameron said.

All the girls agreed it'd be a great idea.

All except for Gretchen, who rolled her eyes in disgust. "You just make sure that revolting creature stays far away from me," Gretchen said, parking herself front and center in a predictably pretentious pose.

A few of the girls standing closest to Gretchen got a whiff of her, looked horrified, and moved away.

"Over here, Ozzy!" Emma called to him.

On the way over to her, several girls reached out to pat him. As he walked by Gretchen, he paused to snort in repulsion, then kept going till he was standing next to Emma. He pushed his head up against her affectionately while Keith showed Cameron how to use the phone's camera. In reality, Cameron knew exactly how to use the camera but wanted to get Keith aside to quickly go over Operation Gretchen one more time.

"What do you need me to do again?" Cameron whispered.

Keith filled him in.

"Hey, thanks, Keith, I guess there is something you're good for after all," he said loudly for all the girls to hear. Several girls giggled.

"Watch it, Shorty," Keith said, addressing his partner in crime.

"All right, everyone...say *Keith's an idiot!*" Everyone laughed instead and Cameron snapped the picture. "Ahhh...perfect! And hey, Gretchen? I think your dress has got to be the most beautiful one of all."

All the other girls looked at Cameron, then at Gretchen's dress, then back to Cameron again—all of them certain they didn't hear him right.

"Don't you agree, Keith?"

"Oh, without a doubt," he said, a huge grin spreading out over his face.

Gretchen momentarily forgot her issues with Keith and beamed proudly, completely full of herself.

"You've surely gotta get one of her by herself...c'mere Ozzy."

The goat sauntered over toward Keith.

"I'll have you know this is a *very* expensive dress that Mummy's designer created especially for me just for this party!" she boasted as she spun around displaying the gaudy yellow garment as if it were a sight to be seen—which it was, just not in the way she thought it was.

"Okay, if the rest of you could please stand over to the side," Cameron directed them, "I'll get a picture of Gretchen by herself in all her glorious wonder."

The other girls reluctantly moved out of the way; some looked Gretchen up and down, several snickered, and one girl came right out and announced that Gretchen's getup was downright hideous. Gretchen, currently even more smitten with herself than usual, was oblivious to it all.

"Our brothers are definitely up to something," Emma whispered to Abby.

"Yep…"

"Now, Gretchen, if you could stand just a little bit closer to the edge so I can get the shot *just* right…"

Gretchen took a few steps back. "You mean like this?" she said, her arms outstretched at her sides.

"Maybe back just a tiny bit more," Cameron said.

"I dunno," Keith interjected, "I'm thinkin' maybe that's a bit too close, 'cause after all, Gretchen's far too much of a klutz."

"*I am not!*" Gretchen vehemently denied, throwing her hands on her hips and her nose high in the air. So high, in fact, that she never saw it coming…

Ozzy charged full-force at Gretchen, ramming her completely off balance. A horrified look shot across her face as she flung her arms about wildly, trying to ward off the inevitable as she plunged straight backward, right into the pool. A huge splash sent water spraying up in all directions, very much like a whale shooting water out of his blowhole.

Ozzy looked down upon his conquest from the side of the pool, party hat still on, with a smirk splayed across his face. The girls quickly gathered 'round, holding nothing back as unrestrained hysterical laughter ruled the moment—with the exception of Abby, who tried as hard as she could not to join in.

Flailing maniacally, Gretchen screamed, "Help, *help!!* Somebody get me out of here!!! My dress!!! *MY DRESS!!!* It's ruined!!! Help!!! *HELP!!!*"

Cameron snapped pictures of the whole situation as Gretchen continued on with her tirade.

"Ozzy! Bad, bad goat! Now why would you wish to do something so horrible to poor Gretchen?" Keith said as he fake-scolded Ozzy while literally patting him on the back at the same time.

Cameron and Keith glanced toward each other in sheer satisfaction.

"I'm going to get you and your stupid goat for this, Keith, if it's the last thing I do!!! SOMEBODY GET ME OUT OF HERE!!!!" Gretchen screamed while continuing to flail dramatically for no good reason.

"Now why would you possibly be thinkin' that I had anythin' to do with this?" Keith asked, not even remotely trying to hide how pleased he was.

He straightened Ozzy's party hat and patted him again. Cameron came over and patted Ozzy as well. All three quite proud of themselves.

"Sorry, Gretchen. I wasn't able to get a good shot of you before you slipped, but I sure did capture some incredible ones once you slipped in and started thrashing around!" Cameron informed her.

"I DID NOT SLIP, I WAS PUSHED!!! SOMEBODY HELP ME!!!"

"Ummm....you're in three feet of water, you know how to swim, and you're right next to the ladder," Cameron said.

Any and all laughter that had died down by this point resumed full force.

Trying her best not to act amused, Abby dutifully came over next to the ladder and extended a hand—even though there was no need.

"I am so sorry, Gretchen. Here, let me help you out."

Gretchen made a big production out of it as if it were a huge struggle to get out of the pool but was finally able to manage it with Abby's help.

Abby's mom ran in the house as soon as Gretchen fell in to retrieve a towel for her. She held it out to her as Gretchen snatched it from her hands.

"I'm deeply sorry about your dress, Gretchen. We'll send it out to the dry cleaners to see what they can do with it for you," Abby's mom said, feeling truly bad for the girl.

"I highly doubt they'll be able to do anything with it!" said Gretchen, glaring in Keith's direction.

"Hey, I've got a great new dress you can borrow once you get yourself all dried off," Abby said enthusiastically.

"Well, I'm certain in won't be as nice as the one that's now completely wrecked!" Gretchen said in a highly indignant tone.

"No, I'm sure it probably won't compare to yours in the least," Abby said trying desperately not to sound sarcastic and nearly succeeding, "but it's still pretty nice. Come on, I'll show it to you."

Abby and Gretchen turned to head inside. As Gretchen—dripping from head to toe—walked past Keith, she stopped. Slowly and deliberately she turned around to face him. "You haven't heard the last of this...I'm going to have Mummy call animal control on that rabid creature!" she hissed.

Ozzy lifted his upper lip at her.

"Well now you've offended him again! Poor Ozzy, let's go get you some more cake."

Ozzy gave Gretchen a sly look as he and Keith headed over to the cake table.

"I DESPISE THEM BOTH!!!!" Gretchen shrieked.

Abby put her hand on her Gretchen's shoulder and looked back over her own shoulder at both Cameron, silently mouthing, "I know you were in on it," to him while she tried to appear stern.

Cameron's gleeful expression remained unchanged.

"Come on, let's get you inside and get you all fixed up," Abby said.

Chapter 15

Gretchen lurked around Abby's room, scanning every single inch of it while Abby dug through her closet searching for the dress she had in mind. Gretchen paused in front of a whole wall filled with pictures of Abby and Emma together, which prompted her to make the face a hapless science student makes when they're about to dissect a cow's eyeball.

She eyed a wall calendar marked with several activities—all of them included Emma. Then she noticed a large, messy construction paper finger-painted heart hanging on the wall, curling up around the edges due to age. *Emma and Abby BFF's 4 Ever* had been written in barely legible finger paints, complete with small smudgy finger-painted handprints underneath. Gretchen looked like she might very well hurl.

"Ahhh, here it is," Abby said, whisking the dress out of her closet, "it's a really pretty shade of green. I think it will match your eyes perfectly…"

She noticed Gretchen's expression. "You okay?"

"Fine," Gretchen said, caught off guard, "but *why* do you have this ridiculous thing on your wall that looks like a couple of kindergarteners made it?" Gretchen said, pointing a disapproving finger at the construction paper heart.

"Actually, Emma and I *did* make that in kindergarten," Abby said, smiling up at it.

"So why keep that stupid thing up on your wall? It's all faded and curled up and stuff."

"Because I love it. I'll never take it down," Abby said.

"And what about all these pictures of the two of you together? Don't you think it's a bit much?"

"No, not at all," Abby said, beginning to lose patience but doing a very good job of not showing it.

"In fact, we also have a scrapbook—which we were just looking at the other day—filled with lots of other pictures of our adventures together. Emma and I've been best friends forever and the pictures and the scrapbook are a great reminder of it all."

Gretchen made a bit of a snorting sound—much like the one Ozzy made at her just a few moments ago out by the pool. Abby looked at her questioningly.

"Sorry, something in my throat," Gretchen said, recomposing herself with a big plastic smile.

"That's just delightful that you and your little friend Emma have had such a nice time in the past together, but honestly? I know that you and I will have *way* better times together than that in the future."

Abby observed her for a long moment, knowing exactly what she'd like to say but decided it'd be best not to say it.

"Gretchen," Abby began, "I really do like being your friend and all, but Emma and I are *always* gonna be best friends. Nothing's ever gonna change that."

"Once you get to know me better you'll change your mind," she said with a ridiculously obnoxious winning smile.

"Mummy says you and I are 'cut from the same cloth.'" Gretchen continued on before a flabbergasted Abby had a chance to say anything.

"By the way, who did your room? I'll have to have Mummy give you guys her interior designer's number. She's creating an absolute masterpiece out of my new room, and I'm sure she could figure out what to do with...*this*." Gretchen held out her arms, gesturing widely at the room.

"My mom and I decorated it, and I wouldn't change a thing about it," Abby said, tiring very quickly of this whole conversation.

She changed the subject back to the dress, holding it up in front of Gretchen. "I am truly sorry about what happened to your dress, but this will look just beautiful on you."

Gretchen whipped it out of her hands, held it up to herself in Abby's full-length mirror, and sighed heavily. "It's sub-par, but what choice do I have since mine's now completely ruined—and so is my hair—thanks to what your best friend's dim-witted brother, his filthy goat, and your little brother pulled. Really, your mom should know better than to let Cameron hang out with someone like that at such an impressionable age."

Abby took a deep sigh, thinking of many things to say that wouldn't be too nice and decided a quick getaway might be a better idea.

"Well, I'll leave you to it then so you can get changed. The bathroom's just through there," Abby said, pointing to a door on the other side of her bed.

"You can leave your dress over the shower curtain rod and help yourself to anything else you need. There's also a blow-dryer under the sink if you wish to use it." Abby turned on her heels and left before she said something to Gretchen she might regret—or worse yet, thoroughly enjoy.

Abby went back outside to the party. The band had started playing again—which meant Emma's mom hadn't yet killed Keith for pulling his latest stunt—but Cameron was plunked in a lounge chair beside the pool, sulking. She went over to him to find out how bad their mom had gotten him.

"So, I take it Mom had a word with you?" she said, sitting down next to him.

"What makes you think that?"

"Oh, lucky guess," Abby said, giving him a sideways glance. "What'd she say to you?"

"She told me if I pulled another stunt like that I might very well end up missing chess camp this year. And that she and Lily are going to make me and Keith split the cost of having that ridiculous dress dry cleaned. And you know what the worst part is? *She told me I have to apologize to Gretchen,"* Cameron said, pulling a horrid face.

"Well, you should apologize…it *was* a pretty mean thing to do," Abby said with a hint of amusement. "But seriously, Cameron, that really wasn't nice. At all."

"Hey, blame Keith. I'm just an innocent little kid, remember?" Cameron said.

"Mhmmm…the heck you are. Emma and I watched the two of you plotting together before it happened."

"Well, see? This proves Keith and I are not responsible. You two had a duty to save us from ourselves and you failed," Cameron said, quite pleased with himself.

Abby shook her head and laughed. "Have you seen Emma anywhere?" she said looking around.

"Yeah, she's over there helping mom clear up some cups and plates and stuff," he said, pointing toward the cake table.

"Thanks. And could you at least try to stay out of trouble for the rest of the party?"

"Why, of course…" Cameron said, sitting up with a sudden mischievous twinkle in his eye.

"Remember what mom said…I know how much you'd hate to miss chess camp."

Cameron sighed and slunk back down in the chair. "Yeah, yeah, yeah…"

Abby walked over to where Emma was tossing the last of the cake crumb laden party plates into the garbage bin.

"Emma, can I talk to you about something for a moment?" she asked.

"Of course. But oh my goodness, can you believe Keith and Cameron pulled that off? I know it was wrong, but it was awesome! And did you get a load of the look on Gretchen's face when Ozzy…"

Emma noticed Abby was not sharing her enthusiasm. "Abby, what is it?"

"I'm fully aware Gretchen can be absolutely despicable…but despite that, I'm just feeling really bad for her. She has no friends, and no one likes her. I can't imagine how sad and lonely she must be."

"But, Abby, how she acts is the *whole entire reason* why people don't like her—it's not exactly like she's blameless here."

"I know. But I can't help thinking that if we really tried being friendly toward her and showed her what it was like to actually be a friend to someone, maybe it would rub off on her. We should at least try…wouldn't it be great to make a difference for her?" Abby said, looking intently serious.

"I know what you're saying, but she's a full of herself pill, so that makes it pretty darned impossible to even stomach being in the same space as her," Emma said, looking thoughtful for a moment.

"But if it means this much to you, I will try to make an effort. For you—*not* for Gretchen. I do hope you realize it's seriously underhanded of you to ask me this today…how am I to deny my best friend on her birthday?" Emma said, smiling.

"Good point," Abby said, laughing. "Maybe it won't work, but it means everything to me that you're willing to try…thank you!"

"Just don't hold your breath for any miraculous personality transformations there…she's practically a carbon copy of her mom."

"Well, who knows, maybe we can save her from becoming her mom."

"Maybe…" Emma said in serious doubt there was any way to stop that train wreck from happening.

Hey, Abby?" her mom called. "Come on over and open up these lovely presents everyone was nice enough to bring you."

"Okay, Mom, be right there…" she said. Abby and Emma went over to join the rest of the party.

Meanwhile, darling little Gretchen emerged from Abby's bathroom in the green dress, concluding that since no one else was around it'd be the perfect opportunity to snoop through Abby's things.

She approached the vanity table, pulled out the bench and sat down, her eyes surveying the trinkets and beauty products adorning the top of the table. She spotted Abby's perfume and tried some on. Normally, this particular perfume gave off the sweet delicate smell of wildflowers, but the way Gretchen doused herself with it she ended up smelling like a funeral parlor gone bad.

Next on her list was rifling through the vanity table drawer. Finding nothing of any great consequence, she closed it and moved on to Abby's jewelry box. She found a delicate gold heart locket necklace and decided to try it on. She looked at her reflection in the vanity table mirror, quite pleased with how pretty the sparkling gold locket looked with the dress. Abby did tell her to "use whatever she needed," Gretchen thought to herself and decided that this certainly fit into that category. She fumbled with the locket in order to get it open and see what was inside. Once she finally managed it, it revealed a picture of a much younger Abby and Emma together on a swing.

Consumed with overwhelming jealousy, she whipped off the necklace—breaking the clasp in the process—and threw it across the room in a fit of rage, where it hit the wall and fell down behind a bureau. She caught a glimpse of her face in the mirror, her scowl making her appear far more repulsive than usual. She turned from it angrily.

Gretchen stormed over to the bed, plopping herself down upon it hard. She stewed for a moment, crossing her arms in front of her, glaring at anything and everything in sight until she saw Abby's nightstand drawer was slightly ajar. In it she recognized the journal Emma had given Abby. Gretchen feasted her eyes upon it. Scooting over a bit to get closer to the drawer, she reached in and snatched out the journal.

Her envy prompted her to open it up and tear it to shreds, but her nosiness got the better of her and she chose to see if there was anything worth reading inside. Seeing that Abby had indeed written in it, Gretchen's expression changed from envy to shiftiness as she began to read.

Well this is awkward. I've never done a journal entry before, but since Emma gave it to me I better actually use it or she'll have my head. Haha...

Tonight, Emma and I did a message in a bottle thing and threw it into the lake. It was really cool. The message was a basically a hope that whoever finds it will find the kind of friendship that we have.

This makes me think of Gretchen.

Gretchen paused for a moment, then continued...

She has no friends, and no one likes her. If she doesn't change, no one ever will. I feel sorry for her, and Mom says I should try to be nice to her as she could really use a friend. Not an easy task, but I'd like to help her. Can't imagine how sad she must be. I really do pity her.

"She pities *me?!?*" Gretchen said aloud, highly offended, and flung the journal across the room.

She sat there breathing hard, her heart racing, her face so red and puffed up it resembled a giant angry tomato about to burst. After calming down a bit, curiosity got the best of her once again. She jumped off the bed, whisked the book off the floor, plunked herself back down and flipped the page to read some more.

Something unthinkable happened today…Emma nearly drowned.

"What?!?" Gretchen burst out, reading it again twice over, covering her mouth with one hand as she did so. Her beady little eyes darted down to take in the rest of the page.

She dove off the diving board at the lake, got stuck in the weeds, and when they pulled her up she wasn't breathing. I was there, and it ripped my heart out to see her like that. Uncle Clegg saved her and got her breathing again. Then at the hospital, her heart stopped beating. I've never been more afraid in my life. Thank God Dad was able to save her.

This is all my fault because I could've saved her from having any of this happen to begin with, if I'd just gone back out in the water like she'd asked me to. Some best friend I am.

I'm still so shaken up over this. I can't believe she took a risk like that just to practice her dives. And for what? She's the best diver in the team.

I gave Emma my word I'd never breathe a word of this to anyone, I just hope she'll never take a chance like this ever, again. So very, very thankful she's okay.

When she finished reading the journal entry, her jaw gaped down to such an extent that someone could've easily putted a golf ball into it. She flipped the page and continued on.

My heart is breaking for Emma. No one could ever keep her out of the water—or get her out once she was in it—but now I'm afraid she'll never get back in.

She's terrified of going in the water now, to the point of having really bad panic attacks. She says she's never going back in the water again. I wish I knew how to help. None of this would be going on if I'd just kept up my end of the pact. She told me not to tell anyone 'cause she thinks people will think she's pathetic. Can't imagine anyone being so cruel, but just the same I'll never tell.

And I get chills thinking about what happened to her while her heart had stopped beating—she had a near-death experience! I cannot get over how incredible it all is—it's like something out of a crazy dream. I'm the only one she's told cause she's afraid everyone will think she's crazy or that she's lying. All anyone would have to do is listen to her talk about it to know it really, truly happened. I promised to keep it a secret, and I will, but I really think she should talk to my dad about it.

Gretchen very quietly closed the journal, and held it in her lap as she considered deeply everything she'd just learned. Then slowly but surely, the most diabolical smile crept across her conniving little face as she plotted to use this newfound knowledge to her distinct advantage.

Chapter 16

"Awww…Emma, thanks! I love it! But you didn't have to get me anything else…that wonderful journal was more than enough," Abby said as she opened up her gift from Emma.

Abby held up a beautiful set of wind chimes, straining to hear them over the band.

"You're welcome," said Emma. "It's not a totally unselfish gift either because I was thinking if your dad hung them outside your window that I'd be able to hear them at night as well."

Abby laughed. "I love that you'd be able to hear them too! I'll have my dad hang them just outside my window seat windows the first chance I get," she said, placing them gently back in the box.

"I wonder what's keeping Gretchen…hope she's not too upset about the dress. Maybe I should go check on her," Abby said, starting to get up from her chair.

"You know what? Sit back down…I'll go check on her. Maybe it's just the thing she and I need," Emma said, smiling.

"You sure?" Abby said, giving Emma a disbelieving look.

"Yeah, I'm totally good with this. Stay here, and enjoy the party," Emma said in a reassuring tone, although the only thing she was sure of was that she dreaded even the mere thought of dealing with Gretchen.

"I'll be back."

Emma walked across the patio, went in through the double French doors leading to the kitchen and then around to the backstairs of the house. She paused for a moment, bracing herself to encounter Gretchen and wondered if that's what first time lion tamers felt like.

As she stood there, intimidated, she decided it was completely lame to feel anything but pity for the likes of Gretchen, and she booked it up the stairs. Once she reached the top she turned the familiar corner, making her way down the hall to Abby's room.

Gretchen was startled out of her diabolical scheming by the sounds of footsteps coming down the hall. In a flurry, she whipped the nightstand drawer open wide to toss the journal back into it, but she'd pulled on the handle too hard and the drawer went flying out into the room, crashing to the floor.

Emma heard the crash and rushed the rest of the way over to Abby's door. "Gretchen, is everything okay in there?" she said, knocking at the door.

Freaking out sideways, Gretchen shoved the journal under some other stuff in the drawer and spun around just as Emma opened the door.

"You can't just come barging in like that!" Gretchen blurted out accusingly, her heart beating a million miles an hour, standing just a few meager inches away from the fallen drawer.

"Sorry, but I heard a crash and you didn't answer me. Just wanted to make sure everything was okay."

"Well, wasn't that *oh so nice of you*," Gretchen spewed sarcastically, "but I'm fine, so you can leave now."

Emma couldn't help but notice the drawer to the nightstand on the floor directly behind Gretchen. Gretchen made a useless, feeble attempt to block Emma's view by stepping back, nearly stepping into the drawer.

"Oh, *that's* what the noise was," Emma said, walking over toward it.

Gretchen's face sprouted into a tomato again as Emma bent down to pick up the drawer.

"My dad's been meaning to come over and fix that for her. It'll fall right out if you pull the handle too hard. There we go," she said as she slid the drawer back into its rightful place.

"Was there something in particular you were looking for, Gretchen?"

Gretchen crossed her arms. "That's really none of your business," she said, her eyes boring holes into Emma.

"Well, if you're snooping through my best friend's room then, yeah, I'd say it is definitely my business." Emma challenged Gretchen by taking a step closer.

Gretchen moved in closer as well, glowering at Emma. "I'll have you know that Abby told me to help myself to whatever I needed…and as for the two of you being best friends?" she said, giving a snooty laugh, "You're *obviously* living in a dream world."

Emma laughed outrageously at that, which infuriated Gretchen even further.

"Laugh all you want, but Abby told me herself that she'd much rather hang out with me…"

"Oh, really," Emma laughed again. "I think you're the one living in a dream world, Gretchen…did that fall in the pool effect your brain?"

Seizing the opportunity, Gretchen deliberately chose her words, displaying a purely evil smile. "No…but apparently you diving into the weeds, getting stuck, and almost dying about it effected yours." Never more pleased with herself, Gretchen stood back to take in Emma's reaction.

Her heart caught in her throat, and all Emma could do, for what seemed to be the longest while, was just stand there looking at Gretchen.

"Who told you about that?" Emma finally managed to get out, her voice cracking, barely above a whisper.

"Who do you think?" Gretchen shot back at her, her head raised into the air in smug satisfaction.

"Abby and I have become quite close…didn't you know? She confides in me about everything, including how you're being completely pathetic over the whole thing and having panic attacks about it."

"She *also* filled me in on that whole ridiculously lame story you told her about having a near-death experience. By the way, she didn't believe any of it. But you should've heard her *laugh and laugh* when she told me about it. She's far too nice to tell you what she really thinks to your face…"

Emma felt as if the life had been knocked out of her— for the second time. "I don't believe you," she said incredulously, trying to convince herself of the words that just came out of her mouth.

Gretchen sauntered away to stare at her reflection in the full length mirror. "It really makes no difference what you believe. Now that you have this huge, stupid fear of the water and all, she said she feels like you're a bit of an embarrassment. And, well, now that she knows what a liar you are…" She fiddled with her hair as she eyed Emma's reaction to all this by looking back at her through the mirror.

"Think about it, Emma…swimming's practically her whole life, and it's *obviously* no longer part of yours since you were dumb enough to go and get yourself stuck in the weeds."

She turned around to face Emma. "But, of course, she feels tremendous guilt for feeling this way. Not only are you way beneath her—like you've always been—but you no longer even share that common interest that bonded the two of you together. And now you're so desperate to get her attention that you make up stuff to boot!"

Tears began to form in Emma's eyes, and the last thing she wanted was for Gretchen to see them. She quickly turned away but not quick enough.

"Oh dear…are you crying?" Gretchen asked in mock sympathy. "Perhaps I shouldn't have said anything. I know that Abby would feel *so* bad if she knew…because, well, she said she's always thought of you as her little project."

"Her what?!?!" Emma said, spinning around. "I don't believe any of this! She promised me she'd never tell anyone!"

"Just goes to show you…you two aren't quite the best of friends that you thought you were. Better that you find out now, I guess…"

Emma burst into tears and fled the room. She ran down the hall, down the front stairs, then around the corner to the foyer, nearly crashing into Cameron.

"Hey, watch it…I'm not a bowling pin, ya know," he said in good humor, then noticed tears were streaming down her face. "Emma, what's wrong?"

Emma shook her head, then continued quickly toward the front door.

Cameron followed after her. "What happened?"

She escaped out the door as Cameron caught it before it shut. "Emma?" he called after her.

"Just tell my mom I had to go home," she said, not looking back as she took off across the yard toward her house.

Meanwhile, back at the party, Gretchen came down the stairs and through the kitchen, stopping at the French doors to take a thorough scan of the backyard, then gave a sigh of relief as she didn't see Emma anywhere. She spotted Abby, though, and flounced over to see her.

"Well, what do you think?" Gretchen said, spinning around to fully display herself in the dress.

"It looks beautiful on you; the green really does match your eyes perfectly," Abby said, glancing over toward the French doors.

"Where's Emma?"

Gretchen was caught off guard but gave no evidence of it. "Emma? I have no idea."

"You didn't see her inside?"

"Nope."

"Wow, that's…very odd. You sure?"

"Well, don't be silly, of course, I'm sure. Anyway, let's not worry about that because you haven't opened the present I got for you yet...you will love it. Mummy and I picked it out together."

Trying to distract Abby, Gretchen grabbed the large, exquisitely wrapped present off the table and handed it to her.

"What are you waiting for? Open it!"

Abby smiled at her, but her eyes kept darting to the back door, wondering where Emma could be and why she hadn't gone to see Gretchen.

A few moments later Abby saw her brother emerge from the house. "Hey, Cameron, did you see Emma in the house?" she asked.

"Yeah, she told me to tell her mom that she went home."

Abby looked puzzled. "Did she say why?"

"Nope, but she seemed really upset," Cameron said as he went off to find Emma's mom.

Chapter 17

Abby started inside to go give Emma a call but as she opened the door, her mom called her over to finish unwrapping gifts. As she went back to the table she noticed Lily leaving to go home. Abby wanted to go over and tell to have Emma give her a call, but one of the girls shoved a present at Abby, eager for her to open it.

After the last present was opened she decided to pop next door quickly to check on Emma, but Gretchen got a hold of her and wouldn't stop going on and on and on about all the plans she envisioned for them over the summer. After that, there was a piñata which needed to be whacked. It was one thing after another and so went the rest of the party. Every time she wanted to check on Emma, there was always another distraction.

Once the party was over, all the guests had left, and the colossal leftover mess had been picked up, Abby sat down to call Emma, feeling tremendous guilt she hadn't checked in with her earlier.

"Hello?" said Emma's mom as she picked up the phone.

"Hi, Lily. Thanks so much for everything you did today...I've been trying to find a chance to call Emma since she left. Why'd she leave the party? Is she okay?"

"I'm sorry, Abby, I wish I knew… she didn't want to talk about it."

"Can I please speak with her?"

"Of course, hold on…" Abby could hear Emma's mom's footsteps on the stairs as she brought the phone up to Emma's room.

Her door was ajar so she went right in and found her daughter curled up on the bed staring blankly out the window into the night sky.

"Honey, Abby's on the phone," she said, holding the phone out to her.

Emma's gaze didn't budge from the window. "Don't wanna talk to her," she said in a flat tone.

Confused as this was not at all like her daughter, Lily continued to hold out the phone. Abby was equally confused as she clearly overheard what Emma had said.

Emma's mom walked over toward the window— blocking Emma's view—put her hand over the receiver and whispered, "Emma, I'm sure she heard that. Please talk to her."

Emma shook her head in refusal, not looking up.

"Is everything all right?" she asked, but Emma just continued to stare straight ahead as if her mother wasn't even there.

Not quite sure what to say to Abby, she walked back out into the hall, closing Emma's door quietly behind her. "I'm very sorry, Abby. I don't think Emma's feeling all that well at the moment. Shall I have her call you back in the morning?"

There was silence for moment. "Ummm…yes, please. I'm really worried about her. She left the party without saying a word to me. That's so not like her."

"No, it's not like her," said Lily. "When I came home to check on her, she seemed fine physically but quite upset about something. She refused to talk about it. Did she seem okay to you at the party?"

"Yes, I thought she was having a great time…I really wish I knew what was wrong," Abby said. "I feel really terrible that I didn't check on her when Cameron told me she left."

"Please don't feel bad, there was plenty keeping you busy over there today. She's been through a lot lately, and I think maybe she's still a bit out of sorts. Hopefully, she'll be feeling more like herself."

"I sure hope so. Talk to you soon."

"Talk to you soon, Abby…and happy birthday."

"Thanks," said Abby in a small voice. She hung up the phone, playing the events of the party before Emma left over and over again in her mind. Emma had truly seemed fine to her. She wasn't quite her hyperactive self since the accident, but she figured that was to be expected at least for a while.

Abby went up to her room and sat on the edge of her bed. Maybe Emma *hadn't* been fine at the party, and she'd been too wrapped up in herself and her party to even notice.

Appalled at her actions, she pulled open the drawer of her nightstand, almost sending it flying. She reached into the drawer and fished out her journal and her pen, and began to write.

I could just kick myself! After everything Emma's been through, I just carried on like nothing had gone on, having a great time at my party. That's gotta be why she took off. How could I be so insensitive? I knew she was upset and didn't even bother to go talk to her. Now she doesn't want to talk to me, and who could blame her?

Abby slammed her journal shut, burst into a fit of angry tears and flung herself on the bed.

Emma's mom came back up to her daughter's room, trying to find out what was wrong, but Emma still refused to talk about it.

After her mom left, Emma got up and went over to her window. She stood there watching the lights shining through Abby's windows. She imagined Abby was probably on the phone with Gretchen, both of them laughing away about what a pathetic baby they thought she was.

Emma grabbed her journal off her side table, opened it up to the next blank page and plopped herself back down on her bed.

I thought nearly drowning was the worst thing that could happen to me...but Abby betrayed me, and that feels a billion times worse! I feel like my heart's been ripped to shreds. She knew I didn't want anyone to know, yet she goes and blabs it all to Gretchen?!?!? I thought she was my best friend...boy, was I ever wrong. And then I find out she didn't even believe me when I told her about what happened? I never want anything to do with her ever again, and I really am beginning to think I should've chosen to stay and not come back at all!

Emma flung her journal across the room, buried her face in her pillow and burst into tears.

Chapter 18

Keith and his dad were loading up their trucks with various gardening equipment and tools as well as bags of woodchips, potting soil, fertilizer, and various potted flowering bushes that their neighbor who ran the local nursery had generously donated as a contribution to the lakefront project.

"It's so cool how involved the whole town's become in makin' this a success," said Keith to his dad. "I think the only people not involved in some way are The Buckleys."

"We probably shouldn't judge them," Keith's dad said.

"I don't see why not; they sure seem to think it's okay to look down their uppity noses at everyone else. Just think about how they've judged poor Ozzy over there."

Ozzy looked up from the bag of woodchips he was trying to chew his way into.

"Hey, Ozzy, get away from that!" Keith hollered.

Ozzy groaned and slunk off.

"Maybe if you didn't antagonize Gretchen with Ozzy every chance you got they might feel...differently about him?" Keith's dad suggested with a trace of a smile.

"Dad, that girl deserves it. What makes a chick like that tick, anyway? Anyway, my major problem with her is I'm not likin' the way she treats Emma. *At all.*"

"You're a good brother, Keith," his dad said, just as Emma came out the backdoor.

"Oh yeah? Says who?" said Emma, carrying a rather large cooler, giving her brother a bit of a sideways smile.

"Wow, you slept in late," Keith said, going over to help her with the water.

"You hopin' that whole beauty sleep thing will work out for you?" he joked and then waited for her reply to get back at him. Strangely, there wasn't one.

"I wasn't sleeping, Keith, I was just hanging out in my room," Emma said, turning away from him as he tried to help her with the cooler as she went to put it in her dad's truck.

"Ahhh...you must've been yappin' away with Abby, then. Mom said you didn't wanna even talk to her last night? That's just weird. I mean, when have you ever not wanted to talk to Abby and talk and talk and talk and talk..." Keith said, teasing her.

She slammed the cooler into the truck bed and spun around to glare at Keith. "I wasn't talking to Abby, and whether I was or not is none of your business!"

"Whoa...what's the matter with you?" he said, taken aback.

"Nothing," she snapped, turning away abruptly as she stalked back toward the porch to grab some more stuff.

Keith followed along behind her, a look of great concern on his face.

"Hey, you okay? Is somethin' up between you and Abby?" he asked.

"Buzz off" was her answer as she shoved by him with a case of bottled water.

"But I'm just tryin' to..."

"I said *buzz off!*" Emma thumped the case of water down hard into the back of the truck.

"Hey, easy there, kiddo," her dad said. "What's this all about" Is everything all right?"

"Everything's just fine and dandy, Dad," she said, not sounding as if anything was even remotely fine or dandy. "Sorry about slamming stuff down."

"It's okay," he said, reaching out to put his arm around her shoulder. "But if something's bothering you, I wish you'd talk about it."

"I said everything's *fine*." With that she turned around, stormed back across the yard and into the house, slamming the door behind her, leaving her dad, Keith and Ozzy looking on. Ozzy groaned.

"It isn't pretty when a female's in a bad mood, is it, Dad...?" Keith said.

"No, it sure isn't," his dad said with more than a hint of amusement in his voice. "Come on, let's get the rest of this stuff loaded up."

Chapter 19

Both Jack's and Keith's trucks were packed full to overflowing with supplies for the renovation work taking place at the beach that day. The sky was a bit overcast, but with any luck it would clear up. Ozzy—always eager to go for a ride—had been anxiously waiting in Keith's truck for at least ten minutes before Keith climbed in.

Jack and Lily had just gotten into the other truck when Emma—who seemed to be back to normal, for the most part—came out of the house carrying one last case of water, which she hoisted into the back of Keith's truck.

"Hey, Emma, hop in and ride with me," Keith said to her, trying with all his might to dazzle her with an award-winning smile, which generally won over his fans but did nothing to impress his sister as she opened the passenger's side door of her dad's truck.

"Not a chance," she said, squeezing in next to her mom and giving Keith a look like he had a serious problem.

"Aw, come on, *please?* I'll stop and get us some ice cream along the way if you do..."

"Ice cream?" Bingo. She was putty in his hands.

Ice cream was Emma's weakness, and her brother knew it. She sighed but wasted no time getting out of her dad's truck and climbing into Keith's, scooting Ozzy over as she did so.

"Okay, so let's have it. Why'd you want me to ride with you so badly that you were willing to bribe me with ice cream?" she asked as he backed out of their driveway.

"Just tryin' to show a little brotherly love," Keith said, attempting to look innocent, which only proved to Emma that something was definitely up as Keith *never* looked innocent unless he was deliberately trying.

"Yeah, as if…" Emma said, narrowing her eyes suspiciously.

Pulling out onto the road, Keith started driving past the O'Donnell's house. When he noticed Abby loading stuff into the back of her mom's SUV, he slowed down and began to pull over.

"What on earth do you think you're doing?" Emma asked in great alarm, slinking down hideously low into her seat so Abby wouldn't see her. Ozzy regarded Emma curiously.

"Ummm…I was just gonna see if she needed some help?"

"Don't! Just keep driving!" Emma ordered, glaring up at him fiercely.

Keith gave her a questioning look.

"I mean it! JUST GO!" she ordered.

"Okay, okay…you win," Keith said. With a puzzled expression, he peeled back onto the road and started driving again.

"What in the blazes is goin' on between you and Abby?"

"I have no idea what you're talking about," she said, knowing full well what he was talking about as she sat back up in her seat, spinning her head around to eye Abby as they drove away.

"Come on, Emma. It's obvious. I mean look at you; you practically hid under the floorboards back there so she couldn't see you, and now you're spying on her.

"I am *not* spying on her!" Emma said as she continued to spy on her.

Keith shook his head and continued. "Deny all you want but the whole thing with you gettin' all defensive, not wantin' to talk to Abby, and not wantin' to stop and help just now don't make sense. Also, it wasn't lost on me that you upped and left the party out of the clear blue yesterday."

"I had stuff to do. Anyway, I'm surprised you even noticed. You were so wrapped up in all those poor, clueless girls falling all over you yesterday. *'Oh Keith, you're so wonderful…' 'Over here, Keith, can I get a picture with you?' 'Oh, Keith, I may just faint and die from excitement because you're really just that awesome…'"* taunted Emma. "Really, Keith…it's enough to make a person puke sideways. And, incidentally, I brought the mail in while you and Dad were loading up the trucks, and it looks like you got another card from your secret admirer."

Keith chuckled. "Hey, what can I say? Girls know a good thing when they see it."

"You are *so* lame."

"Yeah, but you love me anyway. Seriously, though, Emma," Keith said, becoming serious, "what is goin' on? I want you to tell me."

Emma had hoped beyond all hope to distract him from his line of questioning by teasing him about the girls at the party. A long pause ensued as Emma stared out the window at the passing scenery.

"Well?" Keith asked.

"I don't wanna talk about it," Emma said finally.

"Yeah, I get that, but maybe it'd help. You do know you can always talk to me, don't you? Even though you think I'm a pain in the neck sometimes?"

"Only sometimes? You're *always* a pain in the neck," she said, sliding him a sideways smile. "Just kidding. I know I can, and thank you. But I really, *really* do not wish to talk about it. Like ever, okay?"

Ozzy groaned as his neck began to ache; he'd been twisting it back and forth during their exchanges as if he'd been watching a heated tennis match.

Keith glanced over at her as he put on his blinker to pull in at the ice cream shop. "All righty then, whatever you want, but I'm here if you do decide you do wanna talk."

"Thanks, but don't hold your breath…"

Keith double-parked his truck—cause that's just how he rolled—turned off the ignition and started to climb out but got back in again.

"Listen, some of the girls from the swim team have been askin' me why you're not practicin' with them anymore."

"What'd you tell them?" Emma asked anxiously.

"Don't worry, your secret's safe with me," Keith said.

Too bad the same couldn't be said about Abby, Emma thought to herself.

"I told them you were pretty busy helpin' out with all the volunteer work."

"Do you think they bought it?"

"Hey, those girls would buy anythin' I tried sellin' them," Keith said, winking at his sister.

Emma laughed, shook her head, and rolled her eyes.

"You wanna stay here and keep an eye on the Ozz-man for me? It's kinda hot out, and I don't want to come out to find melted goat all over the seat." Ozzy's ears pricked up in alarm.

"Sure," Emma said, giggling. She patted Ozzy, and his concern faded.

"Thanks. So I assume you want your favorite?"

Emma nodded eagerly.

"One scoop or two?"

"Three," she said, giving him a cheeky grin.

"I'll get you ten scoops if it'll keep you smilin'," Keith said, then strutted across the parking lot and into the ice cream shop to place their order.

A few moments went by, and then Keith made his way out of the ice cream shop attempting to defy gravity by carrying three very large ice creams by his generally very uncoordinated self. Emma jumped out of the truck and went to help him—just in time as Keith almost dumped his own triple scoop of pistachio nut, in turn nearly spilling Ozzy's large helping of raspberry vanilla swirl. He performed a near juggling act in the few short seconds it took her to come to his rescue, but it was all good once she secured her own cone while Keith managed to regain balance of the other two.

"Klutz," she said laughing as she took a giant lick of her triple decker chocolate cone.

"Don't know what you're talkin' about…I had it all under control."

"Uh-huh," she said, getting into the truck.

Ozzy tried lunging for her cone, but she pulled it back and scolded him, which wasn't something he was used to from Emma so he looked just about as dejected as a goat could possibly look.

Keith, Emma and Ozzy sat in silence—except for Ozzy's generously loud slurping noises—as they downed their ice cream. They'd just finished up when Gretchen and her mom peeled into the lot, parking right next to them.

"Wonderful…" Emma said.

"Mornin, ladies!" Keith called out, giving them a salute through his open window.

They said nothing in response but instead shot Keith, Emma and Ozzy a collective dirty look—as if they couldn't imagine a more unpalatable trio. They then eyed the rusted out truck in complete disgust, gave each other a knowing look, and simultaneously whipped their ridiculously overdone hairdos around and headed toward the ice cream shop, carrying themselves as if they were the crème de la crème of society.

Ozzy snorted.

"Friendly types, don't ya think?" Keith said to her, waiting for a snarky remark but not getting one. He observed his sister for a moment. "You okay?"

"Yep," she said, although it was obvious she wasn't.

Deciding not to press any further, he said, "Well okay, then…ready to head to the lake?"

Emma nodded, half-listening with a dark look on her face, not taking her eyes off Gretchen until she'd disappeared inside.

"Hey, don't let that chick bother you," Keith said. "She's ridiculous."

"Abby doesn't seem to think so."

"Aw, come on, you know Abby can see right through her just like the rest of us. She's just bein' nice cause, well, that's what Abby does."

"Yeah, good ole Saint Abby," Emma said, glowering.

"You *sure* you don't wanna talk about it?" Keith asked.

"Very sure," she said. "Let's just go."

"Your wish is my command, fair lady."

"Oh, please, don't waste your non-existent charms on me, save them for your lovesick fans," Emma said, seeming to snap out of what was eating at her.

He turned the ignition over, and it didn't want to start. He gave it another shot with no luck and then tried a third time.

"Ah, third time's always a charm," Keith said as his truck sputtered to life. "Good thing it started, can you imagine me askin' Gretchen's mom to give us a jump?"

They looked at each other and broke into fits of laughter. Even Ozzy seemed amused. Keith drove his sick sounding truck out of the parking lot and headed in the direction of the lake, leaving a billowing black cloud of smoke behind him.

A few seconds later, Gretchen and her mom came parading out of the ice cream shop and were immediately assaulted by the black smoke, compliments of Keith's tailpipe. They coughed and sputtered almost as much as Keith's truck was still doing. Mrs. Buckley waved her hand wildly around in order to get the smoke out of her face, accidentally whacking Gretchen's cone out of her hand and onto the ground with an unceremonious plop.

"My ice cream!" Gretchen wailed, jumping up and down at the injustice of it all amid more coughing.

"Come along, darling, Mummy will get you another cone." Gretchen's mom said as she put a consoling hand—complete with bright pink manicured claws—on her daughter's shoulder as they headed back to the ice cream shop.

Chapter 20

The sky had cleared and it was turning into a beautiful summer's day when Keith parked his no longer sputtering truck at the lake. The beach area was already bustling with activity as several volunteers worked diligently to put the finishing touches on the big restoration project. Keith and Emma unloaded the truck and went their separate ways; Keith with Ozzy in tow—as always—to help his dad complete the work on the main dock and Emma to help her mom and some other volunteers with landscaping.

Emma's mom put her daughter in charge of planting several wild rose bushes in various spots along the border of the trees. Emma put on her gloves and carried a spade over to the area where the bushes sat in pots waiting to be planted. Putting on her gloves and picking up the spade, Emma immediately threw herself into digging, fueled by thoughts of Abby blabbing her deepest secrets to Gretchen, when lo and behold who started coming her way but Abby.

"Emma!" Abby shouted out as she ran in her direction.

Emma heard her but purposefully didn't look up; she continued with her digging—now with even more of a vengeance.

"Emma?" Abby was standing beside her now, yet Emma persisted in digging, pretending to be oblivious to Abby's presence.

"Hey!" Abby said, finally tapping Emma on the shoulder.

Realizing it was beyond awkward not to acknowledge Abby at this point, Emma stopped digging and forcefully drove her spade into the ground beside her.

"Can I help you with something?" Emma said, still not looking up but fiddling intently with her gloves instead.

Cameron watched the interaction—or lack thereof—with great interest from a short distance away.

"Emma, what's wrong? Why didn't you call me back?"

"I've been busy," Emma said flatly, deliberately resting her gaze on some of the other volunteers as she continued to successfully avoid eye contact with Abby.

"Emma, I know you. Something's *very* wrong. Please tell me what it is?"

Ignoring the request, Emma walked off to grab a bag of potting soil. Abby followed along behind her.

"Please talk to me?"

Emma walked back to where she'd been digging, ripped open the bag of potting soil and started pouring it into the hole.

"Nothing for you to concern yourself with. I need to get back to work now, there's lots to do."

Suddenly Emma stopped pouring, turned around and shot Abby a look that could've disintegrated a forest. "Besides, I'm *certain* Gretchen's waiting anxiously for you somewhere to join her for practice, and we wouldn't want to keep her waiting now, would we…?"

As if right on cue, there was Gretchen, out of nowhere, striking a pose beside Abby. With a sardonic smile, Emma tilted her head in a knowing look toward Abby then continued pouring dirt while Gretchen began to pour out some dirt of her own.

"Abby! I've simply been looking for you everywhere! You ready for practice?"

"Ummm, I'll be along in a minute," she said, looking at Emma in hurt confusion.

"Why hello, Emma. My, my, my…aren't you quite the hardworking little gardener today. Mummy frowns upon me getting dirty, says it's not ladylike in the *least*."

"Oh, I just bet she does," Emma said sarcastically. Gretchen narrowed her eyes at her.

"Emma, can we *please* talk for a moment?" Abby asked.

Emma continued to busy herself by arranging the dirt, again not looking up.

"Oh, don't concern yourself with the likes of her, Abby, she's a sourpuss," said Gretchen. "Come on, Abby! It's going to be a simply marvelous day to be in the lake!"

With that she tugged on Abby's arm as hard as she could, nearly pulling her over, causing Abby to laugh—the sound of which stung Emma like a bee.

"Let's go, silly goose! What are you waiting for?" Gretchen said.

"I'll talk to you after practice?" Abby said to Emma.

Emma ignored her, feigning deep concentration on what she was doing.

Gretchen continued to pull Abby's arm. "Come with me and have some *real* fun!"

"Okay, okay…you win! I'm coming, just quit pulling my arm so hard or you'll pull it off!" Abby said, giving in to Gretchen's relentless tugging.

They both ran down toward the water laughing and chasing each other as Emma turned to watch them with sheer bitterness.

Emma's mom came over, pushing a wheelbarrow full of woodchips. "When you get done planting the bushes, see if you can spread these woodchips…" She stopped short seeing her daughter's expression.

"Emma, what's wrong?"

"I'm *fine*, Mom!" she snapped as she busied herself by pulling one of the rose bushes out of its pot.

"You sure?"

"Couldn't be better," she snapped again.

Emma's mom stood there considering her daughter for a moment and decided it might be best not to pursue it any further for the time being.

"Well, I'll be over at the snack shack making up some lemonade if you need me. Come on over and have some when you're done, okay?" she said, reaching out and smoothing back a long dark strand of hair that'd escaped Emma's ponytail.

Her daughter said nothing but continued on with her work.

After watching it all unfold, Cameron was determined that he and Keith needed to devise a plan to figure out what was going on between their sisters.

When practice was finished, and Gretchen left with her mom—who hadn't helped with any of the volunteer work, but *did* help herself to plenty of the lemonade while she lounged in a beach chair under an umbrella—Abby looked all over for Emma but couldn't find her. She went over to the dock and asked Keith if he knew where she was.

"Emma and Mom went off to get some more flowers…apparently their thinkin' is that the three hundred million they've already planted aren't nearly enough."

"Hey, I've been meanin' to talk to you about somethin'," Keith said, putting down his hammer and jumping down from the dock to come talk to Abby.

He deliberately whisked off his safety glasses in the manner a movie star would who'd just arrived on the scene.

"So just what's goin' on with you and Emma?" he asked.

They took a walk over to where Ozzy was leashed to a nearby tree—the goat's countenance clearly revealing he felt abandoned and left for dead over there. Abby rubbed

Ozzy's ears as he leaned in toward her, eyes closed, enjoying the attention he felt was severely lacking in his life that day.

"I wish I knew…" Abby said. "She won't talk to me about it, or anything else for that matter. Maybe she thinks I don't care about what happened and blames me 'cause I didn't keep up my end of the pact."

"That's crazy, why would she be thinkin' that?" And just what pact are you talkin about?"

"Probably sounds stupid, but we promised to be inseparable for the whole summer. If I'd held to it, and gotten back in the water with her like she'd wanted, then none of what happened to her would've happened to her," Abby said, kicking at the sand.

"Abby, you are in no way to blame for any of it. None of us had any idea that'd happen, and she couldn't have seriously expected you to be with her every darned second. I really doubt that's what's eatin' at her."

Speaking of eating, Ozzy noticed Keith had dropped his safety glasses on the ground, so in classic Ozzy style, he happily trotted over and took them, unbeknownst to Keith.

"Then what *is* eating her?"

"Don't know, 'cause she won't tell me either," Keith said. "Sorry I can't be of more help, but I *am* cookin' up a plan to get to the bottom of this once and for all…and I just may need your brother to help me."

"I hope it works, but I equally hope it doesn't backfire. Please tell me this won't be one of those lame cockamamie schemes you two are so famous for…"

"I can't believe I'm hearin' you think the brilliant plans your brother and I come up with are lame." Keith tried to look insulted.

"Well, they usually are," she said, giving him a bit of a smile.

"Hey, I'm highly offended by that statement," Keith said, giving her a wink. "Seriously, though, I wanna figure out what's goin' on and fix it for you two. What's goin' on ain't right."

"Thanks, Keith. I appreciate it, and I sure hope you have better luck with her than I'm having. I'm gonna go give my mom a hand at the snack shack then we're off to bring Cameron over to the nursing home."

"Oh yeah? What's that little rascal gonna be up to at the nursin' home?" asked Keith.

"He's volunteering there this summer, giving some of the old men a run for their money in chess."

"Cool. Well, you tell that brother of yours to watch out next time he gives me a game cause he's about to run out of luck."

"Uh-huh…well I'm sure he'll be shaking in his shoes when I tell him," Abby said, laughing. "Talk to you later, Keith, and thank you for your concern. I mean it."

"Not a problem, ma'am," he said, bowing chivalrously.

She shook her head and laughed at him, then turned and headed up the beach. Keith found it odd that Ozzy had left their side during the conversation and laid down about as far away from them as his leash would allow. He decided to go ahead over and give Ozzy a nice belly rub before getting back to work.

"Hey, Ozz-man, I gotta be gettin' back to work here in a minute." He reached over to rub Ozzy's belly but noticed him chewing away at something.

"Whatcha got there?" Keith said. Although as soon as he said it he saw exactly what Ozzy had there—the remains of his safety glasses.

"Ozzy?!?!? That is so *not* cool!" Keith said, removing what was left of them from the goat's mouth. He held them up, trying to look through them, but it was hopeless.

Ozzy gave him a cheesy little grin.

"We're gonna have a serious talk about your manners this evenin' when we get home, Mr. Munch Man," he said, looking sternly at Ozzy.

The goat lowered his head and moaned.

"Crazy goat," Keith said, ruffing up the tuft of fur on Ozzy's head. Keith tossed the non-goat-proof safety glasses into a nearby trash can on his way back over to the dock.

Chapter 21

When Abby, her mom and Cameron got back to their house from the nursing home, they saw Emma unloading stuff from the back of Keith's truck. Abby caught her eye and smiled, waving vigorously. Emma glared at her for a few seconds before abruptly turning, tossing her long brown ponytail behind her as she got back to the task at hand.

Frustrated with the whole situation, Abby suddenly burst into tears, charged into the house and ran up to her room to throw herself onto her bed.

Cameron and his mom looked at each other.

"I'm gonna go talk with her," Cameron's mom said.

Cameron nodded and watched Emma as she continued to unload things from the truck. He decided to take a walk over.

"Hey, Emma," he said as he made his way across the lawn.

"Oh, hey, Cameron. How's it going?"

"I'm fine. Abby, not so much."

"Gee, that's too bad," she said, injecting her statement a heavy dose of sarcasm.

"*Why* are you acting like this?" Cameron said, trying to get right to the point.

"Why don't you go ask your sister! She just *loves* to provide people with all sorts of information!" she snapped, then ran off toward her house.

"Women," sighed Cameron.

Abby's mom knocked lightly on her daughter's door. "Can I come in?"

"Yep."

As her mom opened the door, Abby sprung up off the bed and ran over for a hug.

"Abby, what's wrong?" she said. They walked back to her bed and sat down.

"Emma hates me! "

"Of course, she doesn't. What makes you think that?"

"Yeah, she does, Mom. And I don't just think it, I *know* it. I should've been with her that day in the water, but I wasn't because I'm an idiot and now she blames me. She hates my guts even further still 'cause I've been just about as inconsiderate as I could possibly be. All the while she was still upset and needed me to be there for her. I was going to practice and whopping it up at my party. No wonder she left that day. I don't blame her for hating me!" she said, and after getting it all out she began to cry all over again.

Her mom put her arms around her and rested her head on Abby's, trying to comfort her, but it wasn't working in the least.

Cameron overheard the conversation from the hall and stuck his head through the doorway. 'Can I come in?"

Abby nodded and wiped at her tears.

"There's totally no way Emma blames you, and you've been super nice to her since it happened so it's not that either. I've got no clue what's bothering her, but I'd bet anything *Wretched Gretchen's* behind it."

"You shouldn't call her that," Abby said.

"Why not? If the shoe fits. Besides, she'd love nothing better than seeing you and Emma hate each other. I *know* she's got something to do with this," Cameron said.

"You're wrong, Cameron. It's my fault, *not* Gretchen's. You shouldn't be so quick to pin the blame on her. She's really been very nice to me these past few days."

"How can you be that blind? *Of course,* she's been nice to you…she wants to wiggle her way into your good graces and replace Emma. I know you've got this whole 'save Gretchen' thing going on in hopes you can change her, but it's not gonna work. She's pure evil!"

"It has nothing to do with her! It's all my fault, and now Emma hates me and always will!"

Abby jumped up from the bed, stormed out of her room and slammed the door behind her.

"Why does she stick up for that witch?" Cameron asked.

"Cameron, be nice…your sister's just got a big heart, and she's just trying to help Gretchen become a better person. There's no harm in that."

"The heck there isn't…if you ask me, there's *a lot* of harm in it—*she's singlehandedly ruining Abby and Emma's friendship!* That girl's trouble!"

"Cameron you don't know that, maybe you should try cutting her some slack?"

"This is unbelievable. Mom, *please* don't tell me you're getting sucked into this whole Gretchen thing too?"

Not waiting for an answer, Cameron flung open the door, stalked out into the hall and slammed it shut behind him.

Stunned, Elaine sat there staring at the door, wishing she knew what was going on between Abby and Emma, why Cameron was so adamant that Gretchen was behind it, and who on earth were these volatile door-slamming kids and what had they done with her real children?

Chapter 22

The next day Keith invited Cameron over for what he called a "chess showdown." Cameron readily agreed, telling Keith he'd better be prepared to shed whatever small amount of dignity he had.

When Cameron arrived, they set up the chess board on the living room coffee table along with a wide variety of junk food as they'd decided to make an entire afternoon of it—or at least that was their plan.

"You *do* realize you won't win, don't you?" Cameron said, observing Keith's determination as he set up his chess pieces. "But I do have to commend you on your bravery."

"Whaddya mean?" Keith asked, concentrating so hard on what he was doing that he was squinting like an old lady threading a needle.

"Because I destroy you every single time we play…and to think I'm only ten. What would all your adoring fans think if they knew some little kid half your age makes you cry every time you play him in chess?" Cameron said, smiling slyly.

"Hey, it was just that one time…and that was only 'cause you killed me for like the tenth time that day."

"Yeah, in about half an hour's time," said Cameron.

"Watch it, runt," Keith said smiling.

"Oh, by the way, did I tell you Gretchen's mom called animal control on Ozzy?"

Ozzy lifted his head up in high goat alert.

"Get out," Cameron said, his eyes wide. "What happened?"

"Nothin' except it scared the bejeebers out of me when he showed up at the door. But Dad knew the guy, so it was all good. We told him what happened and you know what he said?"

"No, what?"

"He said if Ozzy ever did anythin' like that again we should get it on video 'cause he'd think it'd be a hoot to watch."

They both cracked up. Looking satisfied with himself, Ozzy put his head back down.

"Wow, what a relief!" Cameron said.

"Yeah, I know. Then he patted Ozzy on the head, called him a good goat and left."

He reached out to grab his root beer but knocked it over instead, sending fizzy brown liquid spewing out all over the beige carpet. Ozzy took that as a cue to instantly jump down from the couch and started slurping it up. Paying no attention to the colossal mess he'd just created, Keith enabled himself to chomp chips with one hand while continuing to set up his chess pieces with the other.

"Ummm…aren't you gonna pick that up?" Cameron asked.

"Dude, that's what Ozzy's for."

Cameron shook his head and laughed. "Emma's right about you. You really *are* becoming a slob."

"Am not," Keith said, chewing with his mouth wide open, giving Cameron a full unobstructed view of the chip mashing event taking place in his mouth as potato chip crumbs accumulated all over Keith's side of the game board.

"Really?" Cameron said, gesturing to the crumbs.

"Oooops…sorry 'bout that," said Keith as he proceeded to swoop the crumbs off the board and down onto Ozzy.

The goat looked up, eyed him in an annoyed fashion, then went back to slurping root beer out of the rug fibers.

"By the way, your queen goes *here*, not *there*," Cameron pointed out, smirking as he took the liberty of moving it from the spot where Keith had positioned it to where it actually belonged.

"Huh? Oh…uh yeah, I knew that."

"*Sure* you did."

"I did. I was just tryin' to see if you were payin' attention," Keith said, smiling brightly.

"Yeah, right," Cameron said laughing at him.

"What, do you think I'm some kind of an idiot?"

Cameron smirked.

"Have you gotten any more cards from your secret admirer lately?"

"Yep, two more," Keith said.

"Wow, things are getting pretty serious," Cameron said, laughing. "Any idea who they're from?"

"Nope."

"What do they say?"

"A bunch of dumb, mushy girl stuff. Actually, I let Ozzy rip 'em to shreds. He thoroughly enjoys it."

They both laughed.

"So you ready to get annihilated now or what?" said Cameron.

"Bring it on, you little rascal."

Cameron moved his king's pawn out two spaces. Keith, already perplexed, waited until summer turned into winter and then back into summer again before duplicating Cameron's move.

Cameron picked up one of his bishops and moved it out. "Hey, where's Emma?"

"What, I'm not good enough competition for you?"

"No you're not, but that's not why I'm asking."

"She's up there held up in her room," Keith said, pointing a thumb up toward the staircase. "In fact, she's *always* up in her room these days. Not like her at all."

"She say anything to you about what her deal is with Abby?" Cameron asked.

Ozzy finished licking what he could off the rug and then he and his sticky hooves jumped back up on the couch and made himself comfortable.

"Nope," Keith said, contemplating his next move, "she won't even talk about it. It don't make no sense either, cause I've never seen them at odds before."

Keith moved another pawn out, then grimaced. "Aw, darn it, can I take that back?"

"Fraid not, loser," said Cameron, moving his bishop again.

"Abby's super upset about the whole thing. She thinks what happened to Emma that day is all her fault for breaking that stupid girlish pact they made to be together every second of the summer, and she further thinks that she's been a seriously terrible friend to her ever since. So now she's convinced Emma blames her for everything."

"That's hogwash!" Keith said, reaching for more chips, "Abby's been nothin' but awesome to Emma."

"I know that, and you know that, but try telling Abby that. And seriously? I think *Wretched Gretchen* has her nasty little mitts involved in all of it."

"Wouldn't doubt it, that girl's a monster," Keith said as he picked up another chess piece.

He paused for a moment, looking as if actually struck by deep thought, put his piece back down and stood up. "Cameron, my boy? It is officially our mission in life to get Abby and Emma together and make them sort this out!"

"And just how do you think we're gonna pull *that* off?"

Keith walked over to the window facing Cameron's house as a slow, devious grin formed on his face. "Is Abby home?"

"Uh, yeah…I think so. Why?"

"Call her," Keith said." Call her and tell her that…tell her Mom needs her help with something over here in the basement."

"Is your mom even home right now?"

"No, she went to the store, but Abby doesn't need to know that."

"So why tell her that?" Cameron said, looking at Keith as though he had three heads.

With a gleam in his eye Keith turned back around to face Cameron. "To get her over here so she and Emma can sort this out."

"As if. You're forgetting one kinda important detail here, Einstein…your sister wants *nothing* to do with Abby."

"Yeah, but she won't have any other choice," Keith said sitting back down on the couch, his face aglow with mischief.

"I'll tell Emma Mom needs her help in the basement, and she needs her to go down there and wait for her. If all goes accordin' to plan, Emma will be in the basement waitin' for Mom when Abby arrives and then we'll also send Abby down there. After that, we'll lock 'em both down there till they straighten this all out once and for all! It's gonna be epic!" Keith said, smiling broadly at Cameron.

Cameron stood up and began to pace. Keith got up and paced behind him. Cameron swung around to face Keith, almost running into him.

"You do realize that if this doesn't work we're both dead meat," said Cameron, a mix of both fear and excitement in his eyes.

"Well, those are the chance we'll have to take, right Ozzman?" Ozzy buried his head behind his still sticky hooves and groaned.

"See?" Cameron said, gesturing toward the goat. "Even Ozzy thinks it's a bad idea."

"Extreme circumstances call for extreme measures, my boy."

"Okay, okay…just quit calling me *'my boy'*—it's creepy. This won't be pretty if it goes bad."

Keith reached into his vest pocket, took out his phone and handed it to Cameron. Cameron hesitated before taking it, then reluctantly dialed his house. To both his elation and utter horror Abby picked up instantly.

"Hello?"

"Uhhhh…hey, sis!" Cameron said, swallowing hard. "Keith's mom wants you to come over and help her with something in the basement."

"Umm…sure, I guess," Abby said, sounding as though she thought it wasa bit strange. "What does she need help with?"

Cameron paused, desperately trying to think of what to say. He covered the mouthpiece and whispered as much to Keith who shrugged and was no help whatsoever.

"Cameron? *Hello?*"

"Oh…ummm, hi!" Uh, how the heck should I know, she just wants you to come over and help her."

"Okayyy…tell her I'll be over in just a few minutes," she said.

Cameron gave Keith a devious smile punctuated with a nerdy thumbs up. Keith shot up the stairs to talk to his sister. A moment later, Keith and Emma came down the stairs.

"Hey, Cameron, how's it going?" she said as he stood at the bottom of the stairs, grinning from ear to ear like an idiot.

"So, Keith, what exactly was it Mom wants my help with in the basement?" Emma said, looking back and forth between Keith and Cameron who both had the unmistakable look of being up to something.

"How should *I* know? Nobody ever tells me nothin'. All I know is she said she wanted you to go down and wait for her, and she'd be along in a couple minutes."

"Okayyy…well that's just weird. I guess I'll go wait in the basement for her then," Emma said, heading toward the basement door.

"Awesome!" Keith said.

"Huh?" she said, stopping to look back at him.

"Uh, I meant that's really awesome that you're nice enough to help Mom." Keith strived hard to look like he wasn't instigating mischief.

Emma narrowed her eyes at him. "Is there something going on I should know about?"

"Absolutely not! I'll get the door for you, it's the least I can do," Keith said as he dashed past her and opened the basement door.

She peered at him once more then headed down the stairs. Keith quickly shut the door behind her.

Just then, the doorbell rang. Keith flew across the kitchen and into the living room to answer it. Abby was a bit startled at how fast it swung open.

"Hey, Abby! Wow, it is just *so* amazingly fantastic to see you!" said Keith, smiling a huge plastic smile.

"Umm… hi, Keith. You see me every day," she said, a bit creeped out. "Where's your mom, down in the basement?"

"Yep, she sure is…she's right down there waiting for you. That's just where good ole Mom is, right down there in the basement. Isn't she, Cameron…?"

"She sure is! She's totally down there in the basement!" Cameron said as he, Keith, and Ozzy—the devious threesome— stood side by side grinning broadly.

Abby raised her eyebrows at them.

"Well, all righty then. I'll just go ahead down."

"Great!" Cameron and Keith chimed in unison.

She eyed them for a moment, surmised they both had definite problems, and made her way toward the basement door. Keith rushed over to open it for her just as he'd done for his sister.

"Wow, such service," she said, looking at him a bit suspiciously. He tipped an invisible hat to her.

"Anythin' for you, my lady!" he said.

Abby felt creeped out all over again.

He waited until Abby was about halfway down the stairs to shut and lock the basement door behind her.

"*YES!*" Keith exclaimed, high-fiving Cameron. "We pulled it off! This is so awesome!"

"Yeah, well hold your excitement there cause if this doesn't work, we won't live to see tomorrow."

Keith, Cameron, and Ozzy simultaneously took a few steps back. They looked uncomfortably toward the basement door as if at any moment rabid creatures from beyond might bust through and ripped them to shreds.

Abby reached the bottom of the stairs and noticed Emma was down there, facing away from her and going through a basket of laundry.

"Hey, Mom, have you seen my pink hoodie? It's not down here anywhere." Emma turned around to face her mom, highly surprised and taken aback to see Abby standing there instead.

"What do you think *you're* doing here?!?!" she hissed.

"Uh, I came over to help your mom," she said, her heart racing.

"Why in the world would she need *your* help? *I* was going to help her!" she said, looking daggers at Abby.

"Wait a darned minute, Mom's at the store. Why didn't I see this coming—it's a setup! *I'm gonna kill him!*"

She stormed passed Abby and headed up the basement stairs. Emma turned the knob, finding the door locked. "*I knew it!*"

Keith, Cameron and Ozzy who had boldly moved back toward the door, pressing their ears up against it for a better listen, shot back away from door as if they'd been launched by cannons when they heard Emma at the top of the stairs.

She banged furiously at the door. "KEITH?!?! *Keith!!!* Open this door. *NOW!!!* Keith, I mean it!"

"We're dead," said Cameron.

"We're totally dead," agreed Keith, fearing for his life.

Ozzy gulped.

The banging and the crazed screaming continued as the backdoor swung open and in came Keith's mom, lugging bags of groceries. She sighed.

"Keith? What have you done this time and why is your sister screaming to be let out of the basement?" she said putting down her groceries, seeming far calmer than most moms would be in such a situation as she was accustomed to her son perpetually pulling hair-brained pranks.

"Uh, nothin', Mom," Keith said, smiling weakly. He could already smell the scent of his doom wafting through the air as the knocking and demands to be let out continued.

"Then why is your sister locked in the basement and screaming to get out?"

"Oh, it's not just her, Mrs. Rhodes. Abby's also down there," Cameron informed her. Keith shot him a look, and Cameron shrugged.

Keith's mom sighed once more. "Let them out...this instance."

"But they're gonna kill us!" Keith said, his sad, meaningless existence flashing before his eyes.

She strategically raised an eyebrow for effect, shooting him a look that said, *"I mean business,"* which all moms have up their sleeves, ready and waiting for situations just like this.

Realizing his fate was sealed, Keith crept to the door, turned the lock as quietly as he could, then made a break for it with Cameron and Ozzy scrambling close behind. They weren't quick enough, however, as Emma instantly burst through the door.

"*WHERE IS HE!!!*" Emma roared.

She spotted him in the living room—looking much like a deer caught in the headlights of an oncoming bus. She marched over to him, her eyes blazing with fury. Cameron quickly ducked behind Keith, and Ozzy ducked behind Cameron.

"*HOW COULD YOU!!!!*" she bellowed at him.

Just as the three cowering culprits braced for the worst, Emma burst into tears, fled up the stairs and into her room, slamming the door behind her.

Keith stood back up to his full height and did an exaggerated swipe of his brow.

"Phew, now that was close!" he said.

His mom shot him another look as Abby emerged from the basement.

Keith, Cameron and Ozzy feared for themselves once more, but upon seeing the sad, defeated look on Abby's face, they realized she probably wasn't on the warpath. Allowing themselves to relax ever-so-slightly, they cautiously approach her.

"Abby, I'm *really* sorry. We were just hopin' maybe the two of you could work things out down there," Keith said, offering her a proverbial olive branch.

"That *was* a pretty lame thing to do, but I understand what you were trying to do and I appreciate the effort. I know you guys didn't mean any harm," she said, giving them a forced half-hearted smile.

"I take full responsibility—it was my stupid idea," Keith said. "It was ridiculous to think it'd turn out well."

Ozzy came up beside Abby and nudged his head up against her in a gesture of comfort. She reached down to pat him, and he nudged in even closer.

"It's okay, Keith. Thanks for trying."

Abby went into the living room to sit down on the couch for a moment. Cameron and Ozzy followed her.

"I'm really sorry too, Abby. It *was* his stupid idea, but I could've stopped him," Cameron said.

"Really, it's okay…I know you were just trying to help."

"Does this mean you aren't going to kill us?" Cameron said.

"No, I'm not going to kill you," she said, giving her brother a small smile.

Cameron breathed a sigh of relief. "Thank you! But I am really sorry it didn't work."

"I really don't think anything would work at this point anyway. Emma just hates me—pure and simple—and she always will. There isn't anything anyone can do about it," Abby said, appearing to be on the verge of tears.

Emma's mom came over to Abby and put her arms around her. "Abby, I'm so sorry, I wish I knew why she was acting this way. It just doesn't make any sense. She adores you."

"Not anymore," Abby said.

"I've tried talking to her—we all have—but haven't gotten anywhere. She *has* been through a lot, which may very well be part of it. I'm sure she'll come around if we give it some time," Emma's mom said.

"Thanks, but I doubt she's ever gonna come around. I gotta get going, but thanks for everything," Abby said. "Later, Keith. Bye Ozzy." She gave the goat one final parting pat on the head.

"Later, Abby…and I really truly am sorry about all this," Keith said.

"I know you are."

"And by the way, thanks for not wanting to kill me!" Keith added.

"I'd better go with her," Cameron said and followed his sister out the door.

Keith's mom gave him "the look" one more time.

"What? Can you really blame a guy for trying?" he said to her.

She came over to him and gave him a great big hug.

"You're a good brother, Keith. A little misguided at times, but you're still a good brother. Emma's lucky to have you."

"Yeah, try telling her that."

She smiled at him, ruffled up his hair like she did when he was much younger, and began to walk back to the kitchen when she stepped in something sticky. She looked down and saw a huge dark stain on her beige carpet with an overturned root beer bottle lying beside it.

"Keith?" she said, pointing at the rug accusingly and then noticed even more brown, sticky stains on the couch. "Really?"

Ozzy slunk quietly up the stairs, trying to pretend he didn't exist.

"Oooops…sorry, Mom. I was, uh…just about to clean all that up."

"Sure you were," she said.

The look she gave him wasn't quite *the* look—and there may even have been a trace of a smile there somewhere—but she definitely meant business again.

"Well, the steamer's down in the basement. You'd better get cracking with it before those stains become permanent."

"Will do," he said, giving her a salute, relieved that at least one of the females in the house wasn't out for his blood.

"And after you're done with that, please go upstairs and apologize profusely to your sister. *That's an order.*"

Keith swallowed hard, a glimmer of fear embedding itself into his eyes.

"I'm going up to check on her and to also have a word with that goat of yours—I take it those stains on the couch are from him?" she said.

Standing at the top of the stairs listening, Ozzy scampered down the hall, skedaddled into Keith's room and dove underneath his bed to hide. Barely fitting underneath, he shivered in fear as her footsteps approached Keith's room but calmed down a bit once he heard her keep going toward Emma's room.

"May I come in?" her mom asked.

"Yep."

Emma's mom came into the room and closed the door behind her. "I understand you're really upset with Keith and Cameron, but they were only trying to help."

"They need to stay out of it! And Keith's totally to blame—I'm sure it was his dumb idea; his name's written all over it."

"Maybe his method wasn't exactly the best…"

"*Ya think?*"

Emma's mom sat down next to her daughter and continued, "His heart was in the right place. He knows how much you and Abby mean to each other, and he just wants the two of you to patch things up."

"Mom, he has no heart, and I want *nothing* to do with patching things up with her, ever! She means nothing to me anymore!"

"But why? Can't you please tell me?"

"No!" Emma said, getting up from her bed and walking over to stare angrily out the window. "Sorry, Mom, but I just don't wanna talk about this anymore. Ever."

Her mom paused for a moment, looking at her. "All right, then. I'll be downstairs if you need anything…and Emma?"

"What is it?" she said, not shifting her gaze from the window."

"Please don't kill your brother."

"I'm not making any promises."

When Ozzy was sure the coast was clear, he squeezed himself out from under Keith's bed and headed down the hall to Emma's room. The door was closed, so he scraped at it a couple of times with one of his hooves.

Emma opened the door and let him in. He rubbed his head all over her for a moment while she patted him, then he jumped up onto her bed and began snoring almost instantly.

Once Emma had calmed down a bit—which was after a good long while had gone by—she went for her journal, flipped it open and began to furiously scribble down her thoughts.

I cannot believe what a jerk Keith is! I will NEVER forgive him for this!!! EVER!!! And I bet anything Abby just couldn't wait to call Gretchen as soon as she got home so they could have a great big laugh about the whole thing. I hate them both, AND I hate my moronic brother!

There was another knock on her door.

"Emma? Look, I'm really, *really* sorry. And I know it was stupid, but I just thought that…"

The door burst open in his face, and Keith jumped back. Emma's eyes seared through him like a knife through butter.

"SHUT YOUR STUPID TRAP, AND LEAVE ME ALONE!!" she yelled, then slammed the door in his face.

"Yikes!" said Keith as he quickly made tracks back down the hall.

After she got home, Abby also did a bit of writing.

Emma will never forgive me for what I've done. Even though it was a really bad plan, Keith and Cameron were only trying to help Emma and I straighten things out. But it was no use. Emma's always going to hate me, no matter what.

Abby sat on her window seat, mulling over everything in her mind when the phone rang; it was Gretchen. Abby had no intentions whatsoever of letting her in on what had just gone down at Emma's house, although she wouldn't have even had a chance if she wanted to because Gretchen was far too busy blabbing on and on and on about the shopping spree her and "Mummy" just went on. While she sat there listening to Gretchen gush about her latest wardrobe additions, all Abby could think about was how much she missed Emma.

Chapter 23

The much awaited day of Lakewood's First Annual Fourth of July Festival on the Lake had finally arrived, and so had hordes of people—the whole lot of them clad in red, white, and blue as it's just what most people do on Independence Day. The beautiful morning sunshine and clear blue skies promised a day befitting such an event.

The restoration project was complete. Monstrous piles of debris had been trucked out, and equally monstrous piles of soft powdery sand had been trucked in; meticulous landscaping had been done which included the planting of many bushes and shrubs as well as a multitude of flowerbeds and plush grassy areas. A small playground had been erected, the snack shack rebuilt and painted, and several new picnic tables awaited family gatherings. The main dock had gone from being a sinking safety hazard to a solid, sturdy thing of beauty. All the hard work and efforts of the volunteers had paid off marvelously.

"There. Now *that* should keep you from fillin' up on too much junk food today," Keith told Ozzy as he finished hammering a signpost into the ground directly in front of the new fenced-in enclosure he'd made for Ozzy.

The sign read, *DO NOT FEED THE GOAT JUNK FOOD.*

Ozzy groaned and hung down his head about it when Keith told him what it said.

"Oh, don't be givin' me that," Keith told him. "Besides, I'm not gonna starve you. I'll bring some nice healthy snacks over for you in just a bit."

Ozzy groaned further, trying to work Keith by giving him a deeply dejected look.

"Hey, you were right there listenin' when the vet said you were getting pudgy," Keith said.

Ozzy winced.

"We gotta watch what you eat from now on." He patted the head of his highly insulted, forlorn goat as he saw his sister approaching, carrying supplies for the snack shack.

"Hey, Emma, don't ya think Ozzy looks adorable all decked out?" Keith said, gesturing toward the red, white, and blue bandana he'd placed around Ozzy's neck.

She kept walking without even so much as a glance in his direction.

"And what about this nifty new enclosure I made for him—all by myself—so he wouldn't have to be tied to a tree anymore? Ain't it sweet?"

"Don't talk to me," she said flatly and continued by him.

"Aw, come on, you haven't spoken to me in days. Not since that silly basement incident. You can't stay mad at me forever."

"Watch me." She kept walking.

He ran to catch up with her. "I was only tryin' to help you and Abby sort stuff out…and you know darn well that aside from that sordid little situation I'm just about the best darned brother you could ever ask for," he said, pouncing out in front of her, offering her a great big grin.

She stopped walking and took a long, deep sigh. "Well, actually Cameron's probably the best brother anyone could ask for, but since he's not my brother and I'm stuck with you…I suppose during those few random moments when you're not being a complete jerk, you're generally a close second," Emma said, a faint trace of a smile on her lips.

Keith's eyes lit up as he began to laugh. "Is that a smile I see? Does this mean you forgive me?"

Emma looked away for a moment considering her options, then looked back into her brother's pathetically hopeful face, rolled her eyes and shook her head in resignation. "Okay, yes. I forgive you. On one condition…"

"What is it?"

"That you promise me you will not *ever* pull another stupid stunt like that on me again. I totally mean it, Keith," she said, narrowing her eyes, giving him an intensely threatening look—a look perhaps even more terrifying than his mom's "look" when she means business.

"I promise," he said, sounding like he truly meant it. "Now quit lookin' at me like that, it's scary stuff."

Out of the blue, Emma put down the boxes, threw her arms around her brother, and hugged him tight.

"Hey, what's this all about?" Keith said, surprised at this sudden show of sisterly affection.

Emma drew back in mock alarm. "Eww! I can't believe I just did that."

"Now there's the old Emma I know!"

"Just remember your promise, loser," she said.

Smiling broadly, he picked the boxes she'd been carrying back up and handed them to her.

"Thanks. Now I've really gotta go get this stuff over to Mom before she has my head," Emma said.

"Oh, by the way, wait till you hear the new sound system…it'll bombard your eardrums with my band's bodacious brilliance!"

"Wonderful," she said sarcastically.

"And I've got a sweet new guitar solo I'm doin' later; you won't wanna miss it!"

"Oh boy. Well, I'll make sure to have my earplugs handy," she said, smirking at him.

Her smile quickly faded as she spotted Abby and Gretchen having a grand time laughing, giggling and carrying on down by the dock. Not wanting to—but unable to help herself—Emma stopped dead in her tracks and watched them. Her stomach was in knots.

"Emma, you okay?" Abby's mom called over to her as she smoothed out a red and white checkered table cloth onto a nearby picnic table.

She walked over to Emma. "It truly breaks my heart to see you and Abby not getting along; she misses you so much."

"Yeah, I can tell," she said as she continued to eye Abby goofing around with Gretchen, neither one of them seeming to have a care in the world.

"I know how it looks but, believe me, it's not as it seems." Abby's mom put her arm around Emma's shoulder.

"I'm sorry, I know you're just trying to help. I've gotta get going and go help mom," Emma said and walked off toward the snack shack while Elaine looked on, wishing she knew what to do to fix all of this.

Clegg ascended the stage and approached the microphone, wearing his mayor's hat—both figuratively and literally. He had on a tall black top hat adorned with red, white and blue ribbons made specially for the day, and to compliment his show of patriotism, he also had his never-leave-home-without-it whistle with him dangling on a red, white, and blue string.

"Can I get everyone's attention for a moment?" he said.

The crowd simmered down and began to gather around the stage.

"Happy Independence Day! Wow, what a great crowd…thanks so much for coming out. Welcome to Lakewood's first annual Fourth of July Festival on the

Lake!" Clegg paused and smiled broadly as the crowd cheered.

"It's gonna be an awesome day and none of this could've been possible if not for the selfless efforts of so many of you. We've turned this formerly dilapidated beach into a beautiful place where our families will gather and enjoy it for years to come. Can't thank you all enough! And now— without further ado—we'll officially kick off this shindig with that great band who rocked the dock at the fundraiser...our town's very own *OZZMOSIS!!!!*"

Wild applause and cheers ensued—from everyone except Gretchen and her mom, who were completely unimpressed by the musical entertainment of the day—as Keith and the members of his band leapt up onto the stage. While the other band members got into position with their instruments, Keith quickly hoisted his guitar strap over his shoulder and grabbed the microphone.

"Let's give a big round of applause to the most amazing, awe-inspiring, highly distinguished mayor in the history of Lakewood—or anywhere else for that matter—Mayor Clegg O'Donnell!"

The crowd cheered, clapped, and whistled. Clegg laughed.

"Oh boy, thanks, everyone! And thank *you*, Keith...now just how much is it that I owe you for that line of malarkey—I mean praise?"

The crowd burst into laughter.

"We'll settle up later," Keith said, winking at him.

"Okay, everyone, it's time to get this party started!" Keith announced to the crowd, and the band kicked into high gear—and high volume—as the new sound system worked just a bit *too* well.

Cameron stood by watching Emma watch Gretchen as she watched Abby fill red, white, and blue balloons with helium. He decided to put an end to it and grabbed his Frisbee from the snack shack.

"Hey, Emma, come play Frisbee with me," he said.

"Nah, not right now," she said, continuing to watch Abby as she attached a big bunch of balloons to the side of the snack shack.

"Awe, come on, you *love* Frisbee. Remember that day last summer when Ozzy ate your most favorite one?"

Cameron succeeded in drawing her attention away. She smiled and walked over toward him.

"Oh, I remember all right…that goat eats everything. Dad found remainders of it all over the backyard the next time he mowed. But it was all good cause he ultimately blamed Keith for it."

"We can't be sure it was Ozzy, you know, cause Keith eats everything too," Cameron reminded her.

"True," Emma said.

She was already in better spirits than she was just a moment ago—thanks to Cameron—and as she looked over at her goofy full-of-himself brother 'rockin out'—as he liked to put it—up onstage, she found herself chuckling.

"You know what? I think I would like to play some Frisbee after all," said Emma.

"Cool!"

They scanned the beach for a clearing as a family of seven walked by in front of them—single file—all sporting white sunblocked noses in the same exact pattern. It made them look like tribal members headed off for battle in a remote jungle somewhere. Cameron pointed them out to Abby, and she giggled.

"What about down there?" Emma said, pointing to a relatively unobstructed spot.

"Looks good to me!" Cameron said, and they ran over to the clearing.

The two of them were having a great time throwing the disc back and forth and chasing it down. Abby took notice and stopped dealing with balloons for a moment as she was happy to see Emma having such a good time again but sad that she wasn't able to enjoy it with her. Gretchen took notice of Abby's noticing and became anything but happy, and disgruntledly threw her hands on her hips and scowled.

Meanwhile, Gretchen's mom, dressed in a blindingly bright white sundress, teetered her way through the sand in her red, white, and blue high-heeled sandals while carrying an oversized cup of fruit punch. Oblivious to the Frisbee game before her, she headed straight for it. Cameron and Emma didn't see her coming, and Gretchen's mom never saw it coming—she was far too busy trying not to fall off her shoes to notice.

THWONK! Direct hit. Upon impact, Gretchen's mom lost her balance, flailed wildly, gained it back again, then lost it completely, plopping full force into a large sandcastle. Luckily, the castle's construction crew *did* see it coming and made a break for it just in time.

Even though she was unharmed—which unfortunately could not be said about the sandcastle, *or* her formerly bright white sundress, which was now splattered with sticky red fruit punch—Gretchen's mom was nevertheless outrageously enraged as she kicked and thrashed, screaming at the top of her lungs about the injustice of it all. A small crowd formed to watch the event. The band went silent. A toddler began to cry.

"Mummy, Mummy! Are you all right?" Gretchen asked, mortified as she ran to her side.

"SOMEONE HELP ME UP THIS INSTANCE!" Gretchen's mom bellowed as she continued making an outrageous spectacle out of herself.

Several small children began to back away, most likely out of fear of what would happen when the angry beast broke free from the castle ruins.

Elaine and Lily arrived on the scene, and even though Gretchen's mom could have easily gotten out of her predicament if she'd actually tried, they offered her a hand just the same. Each of them grabbed hold of one of her arms and hoisted her up out of the giant mound of sand she'd become a part of.

Cameron leaned in to whisper to Emma, "Frisbee, one; Gretchen's mom, zero."

Emma tried desperately to keep a straight face.

"And the way she was carrying on kinda reminds me of that huge fit Gretchen pitched right after she plunged into the pool," Cameron added.

"Yep," she said, fighting back laughter.

Elaine and Lily got Gretchen's mom on her feet—and only one of those feet were still wearing a high-heeled sandal as the other one had gone flying off and busted its heel when it collided with a cooler. However, not only did she not thank them, but she also vigorously brushed sand off in their direction. Her red manicured claws reached up to find her hair even more caked in sand than the rest of her. She shook her head back and forth the way a dog does when it's just come in from the rain. It was all very undignified.

Once Gretchen's mom stopped crop-dusting everyone within reach with sand, Emma and Cameron slowly approached the scene of the crime.

"Mrs. Buckley, I am so sorry. We didn't see you coming," Cameron said, reaching swiftly down to grab his Frisbee and quickly hiding the weapon of destruction behind his back.

Emma stepped forward. "I'm very, very sorry as well. I should've been paying more attention," Emma said, still trying to keep a straight face as on closer inspection Gretchen's mom's hair now resembled a wig made out of sand.

She glowered at Emma, saying nothing in return to either her or Cameron. To Cameron's mom, however, she had quite a lot to say.

"Elaine? You would do quite well to keep your children away from *her* children," she said, waving a red claw accusingly at Lily. "*They are nothing but ill-mannered heathens! And look at me! My dress and my hair—both ruined!*" she wailed.

Lily raised her eyebrows in amusement—but not in surprise, given the source of the statement—and just like her daughter, she too tried desperately to keep a straight face.

Elaine was not amused, however, in the least at the way Gretchen's mom had spoken about Keith and Emma.

"Actually, Cameron was just as involved as Emma. And quite frankly, as far as Keith and Emma are concerned, I couldn't ask for better kids for mine to spend time with. We are all very, *very* sorry about your dress and your hair, but it was *just an accident*," Abby's mom said.

Elaine and Lily exchanged knowing glances as they both turned and walked back up the beach together to the snack shack.

Gretchen's mom was left standing there looking every bit the snotbag she was. The two little kids who'd been building the sandcastle stared at her. She glared back at them.

"*What are you two looking at!*" she sneered. They took several steps backward, reaching out to cling to their mother.

After a moment, Gretchen's mom attempted to compose herself, dusting off more sand and standing up a little straighter or at least as straight as she could stand given she still only had one sandal on.

"Gretchen? Mummy's going home to get cleaned up and changed. Do you wish to come home with me or stay here?"

"Oh, I'll stay here…Abby and I've simply been having the most *marvelous* time together!" she said, shooting an evil grin in Emma's direction.

"Fine then, I'll be back."

Trying to hold on to whatever dignity she imagined she had left, Gretchen's mom picked up her broken sandal, retrieved the heel, and held her head high as she hobbled up the beach on one sandal while carrying the remains of the other as discreetly as she could.

As if waiting for the coast to be clear, the band resumed playing once Gretchen's mom was out of sight. People went back to the activities they had going on prior to the ruckus, and the two small children knelt down among what remained of their castle, trying to figure out how to reconstruct it to its former glory before the scary beast destroyed it.

Chapter 24

Although no longer suffering the indignities of being tied to a tree, Ozzy stood around bored—and perhaps even a little bit bitter—in his fenced-in enclosure several yards from the stage. He looked out enviously as he scrutinized the crowd. He observed many of them stuffing their faces with all sorts of delectable delights while he continued to gnaw on the only thing he had, which was boring, bland tasting grass.

He stopped chewing as a delicious idea came to him. Ozzy surveyed the cruel, heartless sign Keith had posted, and grinned wickedly. He strutted over to it, then briefly turned his attention to the stage, surmising that Keith was so wrapped up in his music *and* himself he wouldn't take notice of what his goat had in mind to do next.

Half an hour later, swarms of people were lined up in front of Ozzy's enclosure, bringing him all sorts of delectable treats. Ice cream, cookies, cake, corndogs and chips were just some of the tasty treats handed over the fence to him. Ozzy happily obliged everyone who was kind enough to bring him a snack by gobbling up whatever they gave him. He burped both frequently and loudly.

Clegg made his way up onto the stage and waited while the band finished up their set—culminating in Keith's guitar solo—which Clegg didn't figure would take long. He was ever wrong! Clegg stood there for a full five minutes while Keith created noise that could only be likened to a cat getting a root canal without Novocain. More than a few people covered their ears; an older gentleman near the stage turned off his hearing aid, and a dog began to howl somewhere in the distance.

Once he was finished, Keith took an overly theatrical bow, much to the delight of his adoring fans who cheered him on with great enthusiasm. Everyone else applauded—which felt rather awkward and a bit dishonest—but what else could they do?

"Can I please have everyone's attention?" Clegg said, grabbing the microphone off its stand.

The crowd quieted down and turned toward the stage.

"In just about five minutes our girls' swim team will have their first annual Fourth of July race. They've been looking forward to it ever since school got out and have been practicing here at the lake almost every day so far this summer. So let's all wish them the best of luck and cheer them on!"

The majority of the crowd headed down toward the dock, one exception being Emma, who hung back near the snack shack with a look of sadness on her face as she watched Abby and Gretchen becoming enthralled in the moment.

All the girls from the swim team—decked out in, of course, matching red, white and blue swimsuits—were already down on the dock, eager for the race to begin. Gretchen's mom had arrived back on the scene dressed in a bright red sundress, her hair shoveled up under an intrusively large red hat, its brim wide enough to rival an umbrella. After standing on the sidelines for only a minute, her hat had already whacked three people in the head.

Keith went to round up his goat so he could bring him down to watch the big race since he was, after all, the team's mascot. He stopped dead in his tracks, however, when he spotted Ozzy lying uncomfortably on his side groaning, displaying a belly so outrageously bloated it looked like he'd swallowed a beach ball.

"Ozzy! Buddy! *You okay?*" Keith said, highly concerned as he opened up the gate and rushed to Ozzy's side.

The goat agonizingly lifted up his head, burped in reply, then plunked his head back down.

Keith placed his hand on Ozzy's swollen stomach, trying to make sense of what had happened to him when he happened to notice an abundance of candy wrappers, empty chip bags, a half-eaten corndog, remnants of ice cream cones as well as various other tidbits, scattered throughout his enclosure. He also had saw wads of pink cotton candy stuck throughout Ozzy's beard.

Keith's eyes caught sight of the sign he'd placed in front of Ozzy's enclosure. The sign that *used* to say, *DO NOT FEED THE GOAT JUNK FOOD*, now said *FEED THE GOAT JUNK FOOD* as apparently "someone" had put their hooves up on the fence and reached over to chew off the words *DO NOT*. He quickly looked back at the goat.

"*Ozzy?!?! What did you do?!?!*" Keith said.

Ozzy moaned in response, followed by another burp.

"You sneaky little rascal. I hope this teaches you a lesson!"

The goat was clearly in agony from the results of his actions.

"I know it's wrong of me to tell you this, but I *am* feelin' a bit proud of your clever underhanded—or shall I say *underhooved*—scheme."

A momentary gleam entered Ozzy's eyes.

"But that sure don't mean it was a good idea!" Keith said, scolding him.

The goat groaned forlornly and actually tried to get up but found it to be an impossible task at the present moment.

Keith approached the sign and pulled it up by the stake to take a closer look at Ozzy's handiwork.

He shook his head and tossed the sign aside. "Startin' tomorrow I'm officially puttin' you on a strict diet…and I *mean* it this time."

Ozzy groaned once more for effect then shut his eyes as his stomach orchestrated a whole symphony of strange sounds. Leaving the goat there to sleep off his gluttony, Keith headed down by himself to watch the race.

Chapter 25

Everyone—with the exception of Emma and Ozzy—was now gathered down around the water's edge to watch the girls' swim team give it all they had.

Cameron smirked while he stood alongside Keith as he couldn't help but notice as several girls asked to get their picture taken with their "heartthrob" while a few other girls asked for his autograph. Keith was only too happy to accommodate them and ate up the attention with even more enthusiasm than Ozzy displayed when he ate up all the junk food.

"Wow, you've impressed me," Cameron said to Keith as he signed another autograph.

"Hey, what can I say? Impressin' people's just what I do," Keith said, beyond full of himself.

"Ummmm…I was referring to you being able to both spell *and* write your name; that kind of thing's a big accomplishment for you!" Cameron said, beaming.

"Watch it, elf boy," Keith said as he put on his big award winning smile for yet another photo op with one of his fans.

"Okay, everybody, it's time for the race!" Clegg said amid all the excitement from the girls on the swim team as they took their positions on the dock.

"GOOD LUCK, ABBY!" Keith shouted, cupping his hands around his mouth, in the middle of having yet another photo taken.

"YEAH, GOOD LUCK, SIS!" yelled Cameron.

Abby turned and smiled, waving to them. Her smile began to fade as she scanned the crowd, searching for Emma's whereabouts but not seeing her anywhere. Gretchen scrutinizing her, a nasty note of jealously written across her face as she knew full well who Abby was looking for.

"All right, girls, back and forth five times, got it?" Clegg told them.

They nodded eagerly.

"Okay, everybody, get ready to cheer them on! Ready…set…*GO!"*

And they were off. The girls dove out into the water then swam as if their lives depended upon it. A jolt shot through Emma as she watched from far up the beach. Seeing everyone diving in like that plunged her back to the day she dove off the floating dock. She instantly became dizzy and grasped the picnic table in front of her, quickly sitting down. Emma felt as if her surroundings where spinning rapidly as she closed her eyes and put her head down on the table. Trembling, sweating and feeling sick, she tried taking deep breaths to calm herself as her heart beat wildly out of control.

Several moments went by and the intense feelings finally started to pass, and Emma did begin to feel almost normal again. However, this second episode—combined with what she overheard Clem saying to her Mom—confirmed to her that she would never swim again.

The race continued as the crowd rooted them on in fervent, animated fashion, with the exception of course of Gretchen's mom, who most certainly felt such unrestrained activity was beneath her—despite the exhibition she'd put on less than an hour prior. Emma kept watching the race from a distance, and in spite of everything she couldn't help but feel a sense of happiness as she witnessed Abby consistently taking the lead.

"Okay, folks, we're down to the final lap!" Clegg announced.

This seemed to reenergize the girls—especially Gretchen, who wasn't far behind Abby. Emma silently rooted for Abby to leave Gretchen in the dust—as much as one can leave someone in the dust when they're in the water.

For the last half of the last lap it was Abby and Gretchen neck and neck. Closing in on the main dock, Gretchen slipped past Abby. It appeared she would win, but suddenly as if possessed, Abby torpedoed out in front of her in an unexpected burst of energy and won the race.

"YES!" Emma said, unable to help herself.

For a split second, she even contemplated going down to congratulate Abby on the win, but thoughts of how Abby had betrayed her instantly took over. Her expression darkened.

"And it's Abby O'Donnell in first place!" Clegg announced.

Wild cheers and applause erupted from the crowd. Abby—overjoyed at her win—hoisted herself up onto the dock, and smiled broadly, standing on her tiptoes to wave victoriously to the crowd as they cheered her on. Clegg came over to shake her hand.

The rest of the girls also climbed up onto the dock and came over to give Abby congratulatory hugs—all that is, except for Gretchen, who held back glowering at Abby in sheer jealously. The rotten apple apparently didn't fall far from the tree as Gretchen's mom looked upon Abby in the same manner her daughter was doing.

At long last Gretchen plastered a fake smile on her face and sauntered over to Abby. "Oh, Abby, what a spectacular win! Truly impressive, really! Way to go and congrats!" she said and couldn't have sounded more insincere if she'd tried.

She gave Abby a brief, snotty hug. Even Abby could see through the phoniness of it all. All Emma could see from her vantage point was the hug. Visibly upset, she spun on her heels and darted toward the snack shack.

Feeling more than a pang of bitterness, she started making another big batch of lemonade—apparently the crowd favorite—which her mom had said would be needed after the race was finished.

"Thanks, Gretchen. You did really well too. I really thought you were going to win there for a moment."

"Yes, so did I," Gretchen said through gritted teeth.

After Clegg gathered the swim team up onto the stage, he grabbed the microphone again. "Congratulations to the entire team! They gave it their best, displaying what truly strong swimmers they've become. Please give them all a big round of applause!!"

Much cheering and clapping ensued.

"And now I'd like to present the winner of Lakewood's First Annual Fourth of July Girl's Swim Team Race to Abby O'Donnell! Abby? Come forward and get your medal, you've earned it."

Abby stepped forward. "Thanks!" she said, brimming over with excitement as her uncle placed the medal over her head, which hung from a red, white and blue ribbon.

"As your uncle, who's watched you go from flopping around in a kiddie pool wearing water wings to winning your first race here today, I couldn't be any prouder. Congratulations, Abby!"

Everyone broke into wild applause, whistles, and cheers as Abby posed with her medal; her mom videoing the entire thing with her phone while her dad took an insane amount of pictures with his.

"Thanks, Uncle Clegg!!! Although I don't quite remember the water wings."

"I do!" teased Keith from the crowd. Abby gave him a look. Several people broke into laughter.

"Oh yeah? Well that's probably only because they're just like the ones you use now!" Abby said triumphantly as she smirked at Keith.

The crowd roared with laughter.

Keith smiled and gave a resigned, exaggerated bow to Abby, then made tracks up to the stage as it was time to get the music started once again.

Meanwhile, Emma tried desperately to detach herself from what was going on by making up that new batch of lemonade behind the counter of the snack shack. Yet, she still couldn't help but listen intently to every word being spoken and kept a much closer eye on what was taking place on the stage than what she was doing.

Just then, Gretchen's mom teetered up to the snack shack.

"I'm sorry, your name again?" Gretchen's mom said, drumming her red manicured claws on the counter.

"It's Emma," Emma said, knowing perfectly well she knew what her name was.

"Oh, yes, I remember now...such a quaint name. Befitting really. By the way, my dress was completely ruined by your carelessness," she said as she lowered her giant sunglasses down her nose for effect to look at her.

"I really am truly sorry about that," Emma said.

Coming back to the snack shack, Lily could see how uncomfortable Emma was dealing with Gretchen's mom and took things into her own hands.

"Is there something I can get for you?" Lily said as she nodded to her daughter.

Emma caught on that she was being rescued and turned around to fake being busy.

"I'll have a cup of that lemonade," she said, still holding her sunglasses down on the end of her nose.

"Coming right up."

Emma's mom poured the lemonade and handed it to her. "It's on the house."

Without saying thank you—or anything else for that matter—Gretchen's mom looked her up and down. She was just about to take a sip when Gretchen came running up to her.

"Mummy! I'm parched! Give me a sip of that!" she said, whisking it out of her mother's hands, taking an enormous, thoroughly unladylike gulp.

Instantly, all the lemonade that went into Gretchen's mouth came spraying back out again—all over Gretchen's mom.

"This is full of salt!" Gretchen said, screaming bloody murder from the taste of the lemonade, which Emma had inadvertently made with salt instead of sugar while she'd been distracted.

Gretchen's mom also screamed bloody murder as yet another dress had just been messed with. Even though they tried, neither Emma nor her mom could keep a straight face and they both burst out laughing. Gretchen and her mom glared at them.

"Oh dear, I am deeply sorry about that," Lily said, finally composing herself. "There must've been a mix up with the lemonade. Here, let me get you a towel and something else to drink."

"I think we've gotten just about enough from you already!" Gretchen's mom spat out.

"Come along, Gretchen. I've got a towel and some bottled water in the car."

In a huff, Gretchen and her mom stormed up the beach toward the parking area.

Chapter 26

The music resumed and the crowd dispersed from the stage area—with the exception of several of Keith's most infatuated fans—playing out the usual scenarios that families who gather at a lake on the Fourth of July do together.

Gretchen and her mom had gotten over themselves—at least for the time being—and returned to the beach. Gretchen spotted Abby from a distance and eagerly waved her over. Abby made her way over to where they were, just outside of the snack shack.

"Abby, I'm so glad you've finally rid yourself of the likes of Emma—she's not really part of *our world*, anyway," Gretchen said purposefully within earshot of Emma.

Abby caught her sneering in Emma's direction as she said it. Emma looked hurt and quickly turned away.

"What on earth are you talking about?" Abby began, but Gretchen's mom cut her off.

"Abby, *darling,* I want to congratulate you on your incredible little win!" Gretchen's mom said, her words saturated with insincerity.

"Uh, thanks, Mrs. Buckley," Abby said.

"It certainly looked as if Gretchen was just about to claim the victory when you took the lead. Of course, you *do* have oodles more time to practice than she does. But once our pool's finished, look out, as Gretchen will surely be claiming that number one spot every single time!" Both Gretchen and her mom produced the same snooty laugh.

Abby produced an obligatory smile because what else does one do in that situation if they wish to remain polite?

"Mummy just bought the most *amazing* camera to get some spectacular photos of me today—as she truly thought I'd be wearing that medal instead of you—but I think it's now only fitting to take a few shots of you with your medal and a bunch of magnificent shots of the two of us to kick off the fact that we're going to be the best of friends from now on!" Gretchen gushed.

Wishing to remain polite once more—although for the life of her she was finding that harder and harder to do with Gretchen—all she could think to do was smile.

What she really wanted to tell Gretchen was that, no, they would *never* be the best of friends as they had absolutely nothing in common, and no matter how much she was trying to help Gretchen and find some redeeming qualities about her, the fact of the matter was she just didn't like her *or* her attitude. She wanted to let her know Emma was her best friend and always would be—but was that even the case anymore? She was so perplexed that all she could do was just continue to stand there and smile.

"Okay, darling, here's Mummy's new camera," Gretchen's mom said as she removed it from her pretentious red, white and blue designer handbag, carefully handing it over to her daughter.

"Just be sure not drop it in the water as it cost me an absolute *fortune*…and make sure to wear the camera strap!" Gretchen snatched it from Mummy's hands.

"Come with me!" Gretchen said to Abby, pulling her toward the water.

"Where are we going?"

"We'll take the rowboat out to the floating dock, to get *the* perfect picture of you out on the diving board with your medal! I would've settled for nothing less, had it been *my* medal," Gretchen said as the smile plastered across her face didn't match the look of envy in her eyes as she ogled the medal.

"Uh, thanks, but that's really not necessary," Abby said, less than thrilled at having anything to do with that diving board or the rowboat as they were both glaring reminders of what happened to Emma.

"Oh come on, Abby, it'll be splendid fun!" Gretchen insisted.

Abby realized it would probably be less of a hassle to just give in and go. "All right, I'll just go check with Uncle Clegg to make sure it's okay if we bring the boat out."

Gretchen sighed. "Fine, hurry up about it."

A lot slower than Gretchen would've liked, Abby walked over near the stage where Clegg was speaking—or rather trying to be heard over the band's new loudspeakers—to Emma's dad.

"Hey, great job with the race, Abby! Congratulations!" Jack said loudly above the music.

"Thanks!" Abby said, raising her voice, then turned to Clegg.

"Do you mind if Gretchen and I take the rowboat out to the floating dock? She offered to get a few pictures of me with my medal out there on the diving board."

"Sure, if you want. Maybe you should do the rowing though, somehow I doubt Gretchen knows how," Clegg said.

Abby nodded, then looked solemn.

"Hey, what's the matter... you okay?" Jack asked her.

"I just wish I could celebrate with Emma," Abby said, glancing over in Emma's direction as she stood behind the counter of the snack shack.

"I know you do," said Jack. "Not sure what's going on, but I'm sure it won't last long."

"I'm not so sure about that," Abby said.

She noticed Gretchen staring at her and gave a half-hearted smile and a wave. "Thanks for letting us use the row boat, Uncle Clegg."

"You're welcome. And Abby? Emma's been through a lot, I'm sure she'll come around in time."

Abby looked anything but convinced of that but appreciated the support. "Love you, Uncle Clegg," she said, reaching up to give him a hug.

She noticed Gretchen was still staring in her direction, so she gave her a nod and pointed toward the rowboat, which was tied off at the dock. She then headed in that direction herself as Gretchen hurried to meet her.

"Hop in, and I'll untie it for us," Abby said to Gretchen as she knelt down on the dock and grabbed hold of the rope.

Gretchen stood on the dock looking apprehensively down into the boat. "Is this rickety old thing going to tip if I jump in from here?"

"Nah, you'll be fine." Abby smiled at her reassuringly.

Awkwardly, Gretchen jumped up and into the boat, bestowing all the grace of a hippopotamus on a trampoline. She sat down quickly as the boat rocked on impact while Abby finished untying the rope.

"Okay, off we go," Abby said, jumping in.

Gretchen held onto the side for dear life with one hand while she tightly grasped the camera in the other—even though she was wearing the strap—as the boat rocked again.

"Relax, it won't tip. I promise." Abby said and sat down to start paddling.

Gretchen regained her composure and relaxed somewhat, realizing that boat most likely wasn't going to capsize and that Mummy's prized camera probably wasn't in any great danger.

"I truly am so glad you've ditched Emma and become besties with me," Gretchen said in a ridiculously despicable tone.

Abby sighed. "Gretchen, I value your friendship but I haven't *moved on* from being friends with Emma."

What is with her thinking we're best friends? Abby thought to herself.

"Well, it sure seems like she's moved on from you, but don't worry yourself about that, she really *is* far beneath us anyway," Gretchen said, supplying more ammunition for Abby to think there really was no hope for Gretchen after all.

Abby tried to shake the thoughts from her head. She knew that nothing should ever be seen as a lost cause, except for maybe her friendship with Emma.

"Gretchen, Emma is in no way beneath us, and you need to stop talking about her like that—it doesn't do you any favors."

"What do you mean, 'it doesn't do me any favors?'" Gretchen asked, eyeing Abby indignantly.

"I mean when you talk like this about her, it doesn't make her look bad, it makes *you* look bad."

This appeared to strike a real nerve with Gretchen, and the two of them sat in silence for the rest of the short distance out to the floating dock. Once they arrived, Abby leapt up onto the dock, then reached down to grab the side of the boat. Gretchen was fiddling with her hair, staring back up at the shore.

"Gretchen, can you please pass me the rope?"

"Huh? Oh, sorry. Here." Gretchen's toss barely made it to the dock.

Abby tied off the rope and waited for Gretchen to get out. She seemed just about as apprehensive to jump out of the boat as she had been to jump in.

"It's really no big deal, Gretchen. It won't tip, but I'll hold it steady for you if it makes you feel more comfortable," Abby said, reaching down and grabbing hold of the side once again.

Gretchen hesitated but then leapt up onto the dock, looking almost surprised that she made it. "By the way, I'm not afraid of the water—*like some people*—I just know that Mummy would positively kill me if I got her camera wet."

Abby eyed her questioningly. "Like some people?"

Gretchen laughed a bit nervously, then shrugged, quickly changing the subject. "First, we simply *must* snap a few pictures of the two of us together!" she said, holding the camera out in front of them. "I'll take a bunch to make sure we get some marvelous shots."

She took several pictures, and they began to have some fun with it—making stupid faces, getting into silly poses and laughing together about it all. Emma watched it go down, squinting to get a better view from where she was.

Abby's smile faded as she imagined how this was the very sort of thing she and Emma would be doing right now if she hadn't let Emma down in so many ways.

"Thanks, Gretchen, I think we've probably taken enough now."

"No, we haven't. I haven't even gotten the ones of you on the diving board yet!"

Abby sighed. "We'll do that one and then go back to shore."

Gretchen grimaced. "Why? What in the world's the rush? I thought we were having a fabulous time."

"I just need to get back," Abby said, her expression quite solemn as she trudged over and climbed up onto the diving board.

"For crying out loud, Abby, look happy! *You won!* Mummy says winning is everything!"

Abby eyed Gretchen for a moment, taking in everything that she was and everything she stood for, the direct opposite either her or Emma.

"No, it isn't, and it means nothing to me if I can't share it with Emma!" Abby stepped back down from the diving board, quickly grabbing the medal and removing it from her neck.

Gretchen contorted her face into the nastiest expression of jealousy the world had ever seen.

"You have *got* to be kidding me!" she sneered, throwing her hands on her hips in classic Gretchen style. "What is your problem? You certainly don't need the likes of Emma around when you've got me!"

Abby had finally had it and decided it was high time to let Gretchen have it too. She stormed over to her and got right in her face. "What is *my* problem? No Gretchen. The question is, what is *your* problem?!?"

Gretchen was visibly taken aback, her mouth gaping open at this sudden change in Abby's demeanor.

"I have put up with your obnoxious, snotty, rotten attitude and snide little comments about Emma for way too long! You couldn't even *hope* to be half the person Emma is!"

Gretchen's eyes grew huge.

"And you know what, Gretchen? I only became friends with you 'cause I felt sorry for you. I wanted to help you get over yourself and learn how to be nice to people so maybe people would like you. I pitied you and I still do, but it was a *huge* waste of my time and I'm not going to waste any more of it. You will never change!"

Gretchen became so enraged her face looked like it would explode. "You pity me? Emma's the most pathetic person on the face of the planet, and you pity *me?*"

"Emma's not even remotely pathetic!" At that moment Abby thought that perhaps she'd never been madder in her life, but she was about to become even madder still.

Gretchen cackled evilly. "Oh really! Well, she most certainly *is* pathetic and just about as dimwitted as anyone can be. Otherwise, why would she be dumb enough to jump off a diving board into a bunch of thick weeds when she *knew* they were there and then go and get stuck and nearly drown and die about the whole thing!' Gretchen said, seeming to enjoy herself thoroughly.

"And now she's afraid to go in the water? What a stupid, pathetic baby! Maybe *she's* the one who needs water wings!" Gretchen continued to laugh. "And don't forget her stupid story about having a near-death experience!"

Enraged beyond all reason Abby moved in even closer. *"How dare you!!! And how do you know anything about that?!?"* Abby demanded, staring her down. Then it came to her.

"You read my journal the day of the party, didn't you! That's why you were up there so long, wasn't it!" She stepped even closer, her face mere inches from Gretchen's.

Absolute horror overtook Gretchen. She'd gotten so wrapped up in her hatred of Abby and Emma's friendship that she'd inadvertently revealed what she'd done. She backed up, not knowing what to do. Then, all of a sudden, a condescending smirk scrolled its way across her face.

"So what if I did? Who cares about your lame journal and Emma's stupid secrets anyway!" she said in a sing-song voice, bobbling her head.

"You and I could've been the very best of friends, but you chose to waste all your time pining away for the likes of that whiny crybaby. And just so you know? I *immensely* enjoyed destroying your friendship!"

"What do you mean you destroyed our friendship? What did you do, Gretchen?"

Extraordinarily pleased with herself, Gretchen couldn't resist supplying the details. "Little miss Emma tried to throw her weight around that day of the party, telling me I had no business snooping around her best friend's room. Who does she think she is? That's when I told her you two weren't the best friends she thought you were but how close we were instead. So close, in fact, that you revealed *all* her deep dark secrets to me, confiding in me about how pathetic you thought she was, and that the *only* reason you were nice to her was because she was your little project. And it was just so perfect because she fell for it hook, line, and sinker!!!" Gretchen continued to laugh, reveling in the horrified look on Abby's face.

"But you know what? You two deserve each other, after all! And you know what else? *I* deserve that medal—not *you*!"

"Fine! If it means that much to you, here! Have it!" she said as she pulled the medal over her head and flung it toward Gretchen, who snatched it up with her greedy little mitts.

"Take it, and get away from me, get out of my life, and stay away from Emma! You're nothing but a miserable little witch *and no one can stand you*!"

"*I HATE YOU!*" Gretchen blurted out. In a furious fit of anger, she took the medal and whipped it as hard as she could out into the lake, then burst into tears.

Far up the beach, Emma watched with great interest. She couldn't hear a word they were saying, but whatever was going down, it wasn't good.

Gretchen scrambled over to the rowboat, frantically fiddling with the knot but getting nowhere. At last Gretchen was able to get the rope untied. She clumsily leapt into the boat, rocking it violently and almost lost her balance. She plunked herself down and grabbed the oars. In her absurd attempt to figure out how to maneuver them, she flapped them up and down like a deranged bird who hadn't a clue how to fly.

After a short while, she got one of the oars down into the water—but not the other—while she tried desperately to steer. She had no idea what she was doing and ended up sending the boat round and round in circles. Gretchen screamed in frustration.

Instead of watching the 'Gretchen Half-Time Show,' Abby was busy peering out over the other side of the floating dock where Gretchen had flung the medal. She spotted something shiny far down beneath the surface. Abby squinted as she fixed her eyes intently on the object.

Chapter 27

From the shore, Emma continued on in her curiosity and couldn't help but be amused by Gretchen's stupidity. Her amusement turned to alarm, however, as she looked beyond the boat just in time to witness Abby diving off the other side of the floating dock—directly into the same area Emma had dove into not so long ago.

She moved farther down the beach, slowly at first, her eyes not moving an inch from the spot where Abby went down, when suddenly Gretchen's boat shenanigans blocked her view.

She ran quickly toward the water and the up on to the dock, all the way to the edge to get an unobstructed view, but Abby was nowhere to be seen. Panic sat in.

"Abby?!? *ABBY!!!!*" she screamed.

Emma spun her head back around to the shore, *"SOMEBODY HELP!!!"* she yelled, cupping her hands around her mouth to be heard, but no one took any notice. Keith's new sound system was working just a bit too well, and it drowned out her screams. She continued to yell for help to no avail.

She looked back toward the water and yelled to Gretchen—who was still flailing around aimlessly in the rowboat—in hopes that she could help but Gretchen either didn't hear Emma or was ignoring her. Turning back to shore once again, she waved her hands wildly above her head, screaming as loud as she could, but it was all in vain. Most everyone was farther up the beach eating lunch and couldn't hear her over the music.

She looked out to where Abby had dived in and there was still no sign of her. Terror ripped through Emma—far greater that anything she'd ever experienced. Giving no thought whatsoever to her fear of the water, Emma immediately and without hesitation plunged headfirst into the lake and made haste for the other side of the floating dock.

When she got close to where Gretchen was she yelled to her to go for help.

"How stupid are you—*I'm* the one who needs help!" Gretchen yelled back, too caught up in her own plight to care—although even if she wasn't she still wouldn't have cared.

"It's Abby!!! *SHE NEEDS HELP!!!!*" Emma shouted.

Gretchen blew her off and continued her battle with the paddles.

Emma pushed forward with rapid deliberate strokes, praying she'd make it in time. She focused her attention toward where she'd seen Abby dive in, looking for any sign of movement; hoping beyond all hope that at any second she'd see her emerge up out of the water and onto the floating dock, but there was still no trace of her.

Scared to death she wouldn't make it in time, Emma pushed herself even harder toward the area where Abby was. She had no plan in mind how she'd get her out if she were stuck in those weeds. All she knew was there was no way she was going to let Abby drown.

Finally, Emma reached the other side of the dock—the very same area where she'd almost lost her life. Treading water, she frantically looked back and forth for some sign of Abby. She was just about to dive down in, when out of nowhere Abby broke through the surface of the water right in front of her. Emma nearly jumped out of her skin.

"Abby!!! Thank God you're all right!!!" exclaimed Emma, ready to burst with joy, her heart beating a million miles a minute.

"Of course I am! Oh my goodness, Emma, look at you! You're in the water! *YOU'RE ACTUALLY IN THE WATER!!!!*" shrieked Abby, beaming from ear to ear.

"Yes, I guess I am, aren't I?" Emma said, actually seeming a bit surprised by this.

They began to laugh uncontrollably, both overcome with the sheer giddiness of the moment.

"Let's get up on the floating dock," Abby said.

They both swam the short distance over to it. Abby motioned for Emma to climb up the ladder first and then Abby followed. The two girls plunked themselves down on the side of the dock, catching their breath.

"Abby, you have no idea how glad I am that you're all right," Emma said, suddenly looking serious. "I really thought I'd lost you!"

Abby noticed the intensity in which Emma was looking at her. "Why'd you think that you'd lost me?"

"Because I saw you dive off into the weeds and you were down there forever—or at least it seemed like forever. I was so scared the same thing that happened to me—only worse—was going to happen to you!"

"Emma, you didn't know, did you…they got rid of the weeds last week. Uncle Clegg gave us the all clear to swim over here. I am so incredibly sorry I gave you a scare like that, but at the same time the fact that you *were* worried— or even cared—means the world to me! And, Emma, you got back in the water! You have no idea how happy that makes me!"

"Well, what else could I do? I thought I was gonna lose my best friend!" Emma said, smiling, yet tears were forming in her eyes at the same time. She was overcome with so many emotions.

"Emma, I thought you were mad at me because I wasn't there for you the day you got stuck, and that if I'd kept my end of our pact that none of that would've happened to you," Abby said. "But then I found out that…"

"Wait, what on earth are you talking about?" Emma cut in, "None of that was your fault, and it for sure wasn't why I was mad at you."

Abby began again, "I know that now, and I can only imagine what you must think of me, but you don't have the whole story…"

Emma quickly got up and walked over to the other side of the floating dock. Facing away from Abby, she folded her arms and watched in silence as Gretchen inched her way closer to the shore. Abby got up and went over to stand beside her.

"Emma, we need to talk. There's stuff you don't understand."

"Oh, I think I understand all right," Emma said snidely.

"No, you don't, and this whole time you haven't been speaking to me I've felt like my heart's been ripped out sideways."

Emma spun around to face her. "You haven't exactly looked like you were suffering—except for whatever just went on between you and your new best buddy. Other than that, the two of you've seemed to be having a fantastic time together!"

"She is *not* my new best buddy. No one could ever replace you. I was just trying to be nice to her…"

"So was blabbing all my secrets part of *just being nice to her?*" Emma said, her eyes wild with anger. "*Was it, Abby?* You know, I *really* thought our friendship meant more to you. So, please, don't even try to go there with this whole thing about how *your* heart's been ripped out!" She turned back around to look out at the water, fighting back tears.

"Our friendship means everything to me, Emma, and never in a billion years would I reveal anything you told me in secret."

"Oh, really. Then tell me, Abby, how it is that Gretchen knows every last detail about what happened to me?"

"She read my journal," Abby said.

Emma's jaw dropped a mile.

"And I just found out about it. I'd had it tucked in a drawer, but evidently I needed it under lock and key with Gretchen lurking around. Oh, Emma, I am *so* sorry. I'd written down everything that'd happened to you in there."

A look of revelation came over Emma's face. "That day of your party, when I went to check on her, I was going down the hall and heard a crash in your room. When I got there, that broken drawer from your nightstand was out on the floor. She acted super-defensive."

"That's where I keep my journal. I absolutely cannot *believe* how stupid I was to trust her! She told me she hadn't even seen you in the house that day. You must've caught her in the act."

"Yep, I'm sure of it. And, oh boy, she was *more* than happy to make me believe you'd spilled every word of it to her. I can't believe what an idiot I was to believe that horrid girl. I should've known that was way out of character for you, instead of stupidly thinking you'd actually betray me."

"Emma, after all you've been through I am so incredibly sorry you had to go through this on top of it," Abby said, looking deeply saddened for her friend.

"You have no reason to apologize; I never should've bought into her lies, but my head was spinning 'cause I didn't know how else she would've found out. And I knew I'd taken a totally reckless chance that day, and I knew how out there my near-death experience must've sounded, so I couldn't really blame you if you didn't want to be friends with someone so pathetically lame. Please forgive *me*, I wasn't thinking straight and I was too pigheaded to see it."

"I was the idiot, I never should've left Gretchen alone in my room with my journal, knowing what was in it," said Abby.

"Not your fault. You always think the best of people and give them the benefit of the doubt; that's what I should've done with you."

"It wasn't your fault, either, Emma. You've been through so much. With Gretchen coming at you with this—on top of everything else—it's no wonder you fell for it. You weren't yourself, and she took serious advantage of that. I should've tried a lot harder to find out what was wrong."

"It wouldn't have mattered. There was no way I was gonna talk to you about it 'cause I thought it was true. I can't believe how lame I was to think that. I should've trusted you," said Emma, her voice cracking.

"I'm sorry if I've ever given you reasons to doubt me."

"You never have! I was just being really stupid. I've done some way stupid things lately; one of them almost cost me my life and the other nearly cost me our friendship."

They stood side by side, watching Gretchen finally make it to shore. 'Mummy' was there waiting, and both Abby and Emma could feel Gretchen's seething fury from where they were as she gestured in an animated fashion in their direction. Both mother and daughter glared at them from the shore, then spun on their heels in unison and stalked off up the beach—presumably to go console themselves somewhere with a pedicure or something.

Abby and Emma exchanged knowing looks.

"Hey, I've got something pretty darned awesome to show you. I accidentally dropped it when I surfaced. Hold on a minute, I'll be right back."

Abby dove back down into the water, resurfacing a few seconds later. "GOT IT!" she said excitedly.

"Oh, I saw Gretchen whip your medal out into the water—I couldn't believe how *rude* that was! Show me, show me! I can't wait to see it!"

"I don't have the medal," Abby said, grinning.

Emma looked confused.

"At first I *was* looking out into the water for the medal," Abby began, "but something far better caught my eye. It was stuck way down in the mud and took me a while to get it out."

"Well…what is it? *SHOW ME!!!*" Emma said, jumping up and down, waving her arms around. Abby was thrilled to see her friend so vibrant once again.

"Close your eyes, and wait till I tell you to open them," Abby said.

Emma complied as Abby climbed up onto the floating dock. She stood in front of Emma. "All right, open them!"

Emma opened her eyes, gasped, smiled and then looked like she might burst into tears. *"Our bottle!"* she cried, reaching out to grab it, hugging it and then jumping up and down all over again. Emma's smile was even bigger and broader than anything you'd ever see in a dentist office ad.

Abby couldn't help but laugh.

The gleaming gold foil label was still there—which is what caught Abby's eye—but the cork was long gone. The note—now soaked through—was still inside, however the ink had run almost completely off the paper, leaving it illegible.

Emma held out the bottle and inspected it more closely, frowning a bit. "Darn it…I wish the cork had stayed in; you can't even read what's written on the note. It's ruined," she said, holding it out for Abby to see.

Abby grinned and took the bottle. "No, it isn't. As a matter of fact, it's perfect because it brought us back together. Think about what the message said; you'd wished the person who found it would find a friendship like ours. Well, it would seem that you just got your wish."

Emma's expression divulged that her heart had just pretty much melted into a pot of goo.

"You're right; it *is* perfect!" Emma said, tears forming in the corners of her eyes.

"And you know what else?" Abby asked her.

"What?"

"We both survived Gretchen."

"Indeed we did," Emma said.

They hugged each other, both of them laughing and crying all at the same time.

Chapter 28

Later that night, a thousand stars twinkled in the sky above the lake as Keith's band could be heard playing faintly in the background—Clegg had finally had it and asked him to please turn down the sound system, lest the entire town go deaf in one night. Emma and Abby sat out on the edge of the new dock, dangling their feet out into the water.

"I can't wait, it's almost time for the fireworks!" said Emma as she began to vigorously splash her feet back and forth in the water.

"Let's make another pact—an even better one than before. Let's promise each other that we'll never let anything or anyone come between us ever again," said Abby, staring out onto the moonlit lake.

"Now that sounds like a deal too good to pass up," Emma said. "I really, truly am sorry, Abby. I should've never doubted you, no matter what Gretchen said.

"It's truly not your fault. I was so blind to what she was up to. It was a way bad idea trying to help her out."

"No, it wasn't. That's one of the things that I adore about you—and your family—you guys are always trying to help people. Who knows, maybe with everything that's happened she'll look back on it and learn something from it," Emma said, looking at Abby thoughtfully.

"I sure hope so," said Abby, "if not she's likely to always be miserable and alone."

"Miserable and alone…that's just how I felt, but wow, I really learned *my* lesson. I learned how important our friendship was to my life. And I'm so incredibly thankful to still even have a life. But now we have all the time in the world to make up for these past few weeks. Speaking of which, I think the first thing we could do is…"

Abby cut her off midsentence. "About that, Emma. I've got to talk to you about something. Ever since we were at the floating dock earlier today I've been trying to find the right time to bring it up."

"What is it?" asked Emma, concern spreading over her face.

"We actually *don't* have all the time in the world anymore, I'm afraid."

"What are you talking about?" Emma said, searching Abby's face.

"Do you remember when I told you a few months back that my dad had applied for a grant to fund a very much needed medical clinic in a small African village?"

Emma nodded.

"Well, he just found out the grant's been approved."

"That's great news! He must be so pleased!"

"He's very pleased, and they want him to go over there to get it up and running immediately."

"How long will he have to be gone?"

"Six months. But the thing of it is, it's not just my dad who's going, Emma—my whole family's going. We leave the end of next week."

A wave of shock and disbelief washed over Emma as she took in Abby's words. "Are you sure you have to go?"

Abby nodded in reply.

For a moment neither one of them knew what to say, they just looked at each other, trying to fight back the tears—which turned out to be a losing battle.

"I'm gonna miss you so much," Abby said, giving Emma a big hug.

"Gonna miss you too," Emma said.

"Mom says it's the chance of a lifetime for us," Abby said, wiping her tears away. "All four of us will have a chance to help out over there."

Emma wiped her tears away as well. "I can picture you all over there, working so hard to help people—it's what you guys do best. Oh, Abby, I'll miss you like crazy! You and your whole family. But your dad's the best doctor there is—they'll be lucky to have him. I wouldn't even be here right now if it weren't for him."

"I know."

"We absolutely cannot be sad about this," Emma said, putting on a smile. "We've already wasted enough time doing that lately, don't you think?"

"Yes." Abby smiled in return.

"You and your family are going to do wonderful things over there. I'm already so very proud of all of you!" Emma said.

"Thank you, that means a lot to me."

"And you know what? I've got an awesome idea! Keith and his band members are always doing these video chats lately on the computer. We'll get him to teach us how before you leave. That way we'll still be able to see and talk to each other every single day! Almost just like you never left, except you'll have a bunch of cool adventures to tell me about!" Emma said, excitement gleaming in her eyes.

"Emma, that would be so cool! I just knew your brother would be good for something one of these days."

They both cracked up.

"And we need to keep writing in our journals—every day—and trade them when I get back so we can know everything that went on while we were apart."

"I love that idea!" Emma said. "And I have another idea. Stay here, I'll be right back!"

Emma sprang up and ran up the beach. A few minutes later she came back carrying another bottle—just like their first one, a pen and another notepad and a flashlight.

"I'm thinking we need to send another one of these out," she said.

"I'm thinking you're right," Abby beamed.

"Do you mind if I write this one too? I know exactly what it should say…"

"By all means…" Abby said.

Abby held the flashlight for Emma who began to furiously scribble away like a person possessed. Once she was done writing, Emma grabbed the flashlight back from Abby and proceeded to read aloud what she'd written.

My wish for whoever finds this bottle is that if you have someone who means everything to you, you never make the mistake of letting anyone or anything come between you. I made that mistake big time, and it wasn't until I thought I'd lost that person for real that I came to my senses. You never know how much time you have, so make the most of it with the people you love.

Yours Truly,
Emma R.

"That's perfect, but you're gonna make me start crying all over again," Abby said as the waterworks started to fall, which also made Emma start crying again.

"Okay, seriously? We need to stop blubbering here, because if Keith or Cameron see this they'll never let us live it down," Emma said, her tears turning into laughter.

"Haha, you got that right," said Abby.

Emma rolled up the note and place it inside the bottle. She started to put the cork in but thought better of it.

"I'll let you do the honors with the cork this time," she said.

Abby took the bottle and crammed the cork down in tight but not wanting to leave anything to chance this time she tried cramming it even farther still until she could cram no more.

"There. I think that should do it. You wanna throw it?"

"Nope. You do it," said Emma.

"All righty then, here we go!"

And with that, Abby flung the bottle out as far she possibly could into the lake. The timing couldn't have been better, for as soon as they heard it hit the water the fireworks began.

Epilogue

Wow, it's been like two weeks since Abby left, and I totally haven't written anything till now. There's been so much happening!

I spoke to Clem before they left, and we had an AWESOME talk! He said if I felt like sharing my experience, he'd set something up with the hospital so I could maybe bring a little comfort to some of the dying patients and their families.

I've always wanted to help people like Abby's family does, so I gave it a shot. It was really hard at first but worth it. I've met very nice people and when they heard my story it seemed to bring them peace. I loved being able to help them, and I hope to be able to help others in the same way. It also helped me. Clem said it's not good for me to keep things bottled up inside the way I do sometimes, and he's right.

I finally told Keith all about my experience, and he didn't even remotely laugh at me. He said he wondered if something like that had happened 'cause of what I'd said about Ozzy being in Clegg's truck, but he didn't want to badger me if I wasn't ready to talk about it. He really is a way better brother than I give him credit for—but he'll NEVER hear that from me! Haha!

After what happened I really, really wanted to start going to church. So we all started going as a family, and Keith's band is even going to play at the church carnival next month.

I told the swim team about the stupid chance I took and how it nearly cost me my life. They didn't think I was pathetic at all and were totally glad I told them 'cause it made them see how dangerous the water can be, even for strong swimmers like us. They even elected me the team captain! I'm enjoying every second of being back in the water.

I've video chatted with Abby a bunch of times, and they're all doing super great over there! It's lots of work, but they love it. Abby helps out at the clinic every day, and Cameron's even taught some of the locals how to play chess.

And I've saved the funniest thing ever for last: I found out who Keith's secret admirer is—IT'S GRETCHEN!!!! Hahaha!!! Today at swim practice she spilled a bunch of stuff out of her backpack, and one of the things that fell out was a card with hand drawn hearts all over it addressed to Keith! She was SO embarrassed!

Oh boy! Abby and I may have survived Gretchen, but will Keith be so lucky???? ☺

ABOUT THE AUTHOR

Bonnie Daly lives in New London, Connecticut with her husband Tim and their son Cameron. When she's not busy trying to keep the two of them out of mischief she enjoys spoiling her pets, reading, playing the piano, tennis, camping, and writing humor—which is pretty much the only thing keeping her out of an asylum.

Surviving Gretchen is her fourth book, and the first one in the series *The Storms of Friendship*.

Visit her at:
www.authorbonniedaly.com
https://bonniedalyblog.wordpress.com/

Other titles by Bonnie Daly are:

Christmas Madness, Mayhem, & Mall Santas: Humorous Insights into the Holiday Season

The Totally Lame Joke Book

The Totally Disturbing Christmas Joke Book

Prescription for Laughter

Other Books by Lune Spark

On Writing Wonderfully (Writing reference)
(Age: 10+ years)
The script of Pawan Mishra's talk to Lady Shri Ram College, which has since become a popular reference for students of creative writing and aspiring writers.

A Window to Young Minds (Short stories)
(Age: 10+ years)
This book is the first of the Lune Spark Short Story Contest's yearly anthologies and includes twenty-five award-winning short stories by young writers.

Speaking Up for Each Other (Short stories for tweens and middle grade readers)
(Age: 10–13 years)
Wonderfully wide-ranging, original, and enjoyable, this outstanding collection features twenty-four short stories like That Glowing Penny, in which a helpless girl has to live in fear of her own family.

Coinman (Fiction, humor, satire, office parody)
(Age: 13+ years)
Coinman is one of life's victims, the receiver of subtle bullying in an office environment and thinly disguised control in his own home, but he remains true to his desire to be polite and accepting of how he is treated by everyone. Then an incident at work changes all that.

The Emotional Embodiment of Stars (Short stories for young adults)
(Age: 13+ years)
Wonderfully wide-ranging, original, and enjoyable, this outstanding collection features twenty-seven short stories like Mortimer, in which an unwanted guest secretly follows a family through their heartbreaking sorrows.

My Teacher Hilda (Picture book series)
(Age: 3–8 years)

Playing is an important part of children's learning and development. Appropriate for children in the age range of three to eight years, this book series focuses on play-based early learning. The cute animal characters continuously engage in fun-filled activities that help children learn.

Nora's First Day at School   **The Water Balloon Fight**   **A Picnic Day**

The Lemonade Stand   **Mother's Day**